MYSTERY OCCURRENCE

Stevie Rose

Prologue

Martin was waiting outside the hospital entrance. It was only lunchtime and he normally didn't leave until at least five. His car approached and he walked towards it, politely greeting the driver Chadi and then acknowledging his wife Patricia and daughter Emily who were in the back seat. He knew, as he lowered himself into the car and turned to face his beautiful daughter, that today was the beginning of the end and the start of the unknown.

"Hi Dad," said Emily.

"Nice to play hooky occasionally," said Patricia, although none of them felt it was that simple.

The drive was long and mostly silent. All were deep in thought. Martin spoke with Chadi; it was small talk about the weather and workloads. Even in a crisis Chadi could not be ignored or disrespected. Emily stared outside, replaying the events of the day in her mind. Martin tensed as they approached the house. All the sleepless nights he'd experienced over the years wondering when this time would come. The expectation of today was finally about to become a reality. It was the last time his family would all be together in a world they were familiar with.

The Newells thanked Chadi and said their goodbyes. All turned to face the house, Patricia placing her arm on Emily's shoulder as a mother's comfort. It was going to be a very emotional night. Martin opened the door and let the girls walk in first. The familiarity of the house brought a sense of safety.

"OK. So, you both know something about me that I didn't know," said Emily. "I always wondered why I had these feelings about people. I just thought it was normal. But you knew, didn't you?"

"Yes," said Martin, with a sigh. He had dreaded this day; it was the day that Emily would learn the truth. He had wondered how he as a father could look into her eyes and explain the story, heavy with the uneasiness of not knowing how his daughter would cope with this detail. He hoped they had given her the emotional skills and strength needed for this event.

"We knew you would eventually find out. We didn't know how or when," said Patricia, tightening her embrace. She turned to face Emily and looked into her eyes. "When you told us the homeless man would return to explain his presence, Dad and I knew the time had arrived. Let's sit down and put the jigsaw together."

"We'll need a drink first. Anyone else having a cup of tea?" asked Martin.

"It's too early for Scotch, even though it's probably warranted. I'll have a cup of tea please," replied Emily.

"I'll make it," said Patricia. "I feel like a coffee." Patricia went into the kitchen and Martin and Emily went to the sitting room.

Emily sat down and let out a sigh. "Arh Dad, what a day." She was emotionally drained. "I can't believe how my nice, uneventful life has been thrown into chaos and turned upside down, in just two months." Emily shook her head. "It all started with that car accident."

Chapter One

Two Months Earlier

Two beautiful ladies stood on the corner of 96th Street and West End Avenue intersection: Emily and her best friend Ashley. It was only nine thirty and it had already been a very busy morning shopping for last minute items for tomorrow night's Foundation charity fundraiser.

Even though they had both been brought up by the Newells, they were not related by birth and were often mistaken for sisters. Both were tall, had athletic builds and thick, long brown hair always styled differently than the others'. Emily had green eyes while Ashley had brown. Today, both were dressed in classic shorts and casual shirts, with Emily adding a light cardigan.

New York City was always so vibrant, so much traffic, so many people living their life. The city atmosphere was very familiar and welcoming to a local. Emily pressed the button for the pedestrian crossing. "Ash, we may want to step back from the curb," said Emily, noticing how fast the cars were speeding past.

Suddenly, an unfamiliar soft flutter beat through Emily's heart. She turned around just as a man wearing a hooded jacket fell onto the road in front of her and into the path of an oncoming car. Her first thought was the man had been pushed into the path of the car, but a quick glance behind saw only an elderly lady and no one else close enough that could have been responsible. "I can't believe he wasn't pushed," Emily said.

A lady in the crowd screamed "Look out!" as a car ran over the man on the road. The next three cars in traffic all swerved to avoid the first car, hitting indiscriminate people who were waiting on the crowded curb.

It took a moment for Emily to work out exactly what was going on. A car swerved very close to Ashley knocking an elderly man nearby onto the ground. The elderly lady Emily had noticed before was in obvious shock, but still uninjured. Emily suddenly realized she was closest to the curb with no room to move back. She closed her eyes and readied herself for the impact of a car. When all cars had caused their damage and come to a halt, she was very surprised she and Ashley had not been hit.

Emily and Ashley looked at each other and without a word, went to assist the injured. In her haste, Ashley tripped over a bag and fell, hitting her head on the road. Emily bent down beside her friend to see if she was alright.

"I feel a bit dizzy. I can't feel any blood coming out of my head, so leave me here while you go help the others. I'll be over soon."

Emily looked around for someone to stay with Ashley. Nearly everyone was busy helping others. A man stood alone staring at her. He had the same air about him as some of the homeless people she worked with. Was he in shock? She shouted at him to break his trance. "Come over here and help my friend!" He came over but didn't say anything. "She's a doctor and I need her to be OK first. Can you help her over to that seat and just sit with her until she feels alright? I'll keep her bag so you only have to look after her. I'll come back when I can." The man nodded.

Throwing Ashley's bag over her shoulder, Emily turned to Ashley. "Are you OK to walk?" Ashley nodded. Emily and the homeless man helped her into a standing position, then Emily checked again that there was no blood on Ashley's head. The man put his arm around Ashley's waist and helped her over to the seat.

Emily turned and refocused on the tragedy in front of her. She noticed onlookers had pulled off whatever spare clothing they had. People had rushed to assist the injured lying on the road. Handbags were being used as pillows on the hard road and any clothing was used for bandages to stem the blood flow.

Emily pulled off her cardigan and handed it to one of the people assisting the injured. She checked that Ashley was alright and then walked into the center of the road using her cell phone to call the ambulances, and as a trained professional, provided the scene location, the number of accident casualties and requested the number of ambulances that would be needed.

Several drivers had exited their cars, their bodies vibrating with shock and fear. People were clearly unsure with what had just happened. They all bent down and checked the closest injured person. A bystander ran to assist a lady driver who was seriously injured. Onlookers gathered, reaching for their phones to call emergency services.

* * *

Ashley sat on a wooden seat near the bus zone for waiting passengers. The homeless man stood next to the seat. Ashley's headache and dizziness were receding and she was starting to feel alright. It had only been a matter of minutes. Ashley watched Emily attending to the chaos. She turned to the man next to her. "Thank you for helping me. I just need another minute. What's your name?"

"John," he said while watching Emily. He had such a puzzled look on his face, like he was trying to figure out what she was doing or who she was.

"John, thank you for sitting with me. I feel alright so I'll go and help Emily now." John walked with Ashley towards the middle of the road, his eyes still on Emily. The emergency services had not yet arrived. Ashley had no time to think about John's odd behavior as she assisted the injured in order of priority.

* * *

John wanted to talk to Emily. He had almost reached her when out of nowhere, two men ran past nearly knocking him down. They ran on the road rather than the crowded footpath. They ran in between the car pileup and through the people assisting those involved in the accidents. The first man was a young teen and was dressed in the usual street wear with running shoes on. He was dressed prepared for a street chase, yet looked extremely frightened and appeared to be running for his life.

His pursuer was expensively dressed and didn't look prepared for a street chase with his expensive shoes. He had a look of determination on his face and his obvious intent was to catch the man running in front of him. The pursuer kept one hand in his pocket, and John thought he probably held a gun. John looked down at the hooded man who had caused the accident. He was still lying on the road waiting for his ambulance to arrive. He wasn't well enough to walk away from this scene; his day was ending here. He glanced once more at Emily and with obvious regret, turned and run after the strange duo.

* * *

Before long the scene was crowded with ambulances, tow trucks and police. Once the road was cleared, two police officers started to direct the traffic and assist with clearing the backlog of traffic trying to get through the four intersection directions.

Emily and Ashley remained at the scene to give their account and personal details to police. Ashley assisted the ambulance drivers with patients while Emily made sure all the accident victims had been able to make a telephone call and advise their families of what was happening and where they were. She offered her own phone where necessary. The chaotic scene was soon under control.

"The homeless man was kind to sit with me," Ashley said as they walked to a quieter area. "His name was John. You probably didn't notice his looks. He was different but the same as the Foundation's clients."

"How so?"

"He was wearing a torn dark shirt, ripped jeans and smudged shoes. But he didn't look dirty or smell unclean like many of the people who seek Foundation help. He just appeared unkempt and solitary like a homeless man. He was very handsome with jet black hair, unique green eyes and a face of flawless skin."

"You noticed all that in less than three minutes, surrounded by trauma and pain?" replied Emily in shock.

"That's the funny thing. As soon as I started to walk over to the seat, I could feel my pain really easing. I recovered very quickly and as a doctor you know I've been trained to assess traumatic situations fast."

Emily laughed. "We were really lucky today. I don't know how we weren't hit by any cars. Are you OK if I call Chadi and see if he's free?"

"Call away. I'll sacrifice a chauffeured car ride home instead of the train."

Emily rang Chadi and told him the location. He said he would meet them in the next block in fifteen minutes.

The hospital would be impacted. Ashley prepared herself to be called in.

Chapter Two

The racquetball court was getting a lot of action. It was being covered very quickly and competitively by two young men. They had been playing since seven thirty this morning, and after an hour of dedication both had proven they were very athletic.

"I'm glad we made our game earlier today. I wasn't happy getting paged all the time and not being able to complete a game. With all the patients yesterday we would've had to cancel again. I really need this action to unwind," said Ryan.

Ryan Peters worked with Michael Lister at Royal County Hospital in Washington Heights, Manhattan. Michael was a trainee consultant doctor. He had blond hair which was always neatly groomed. His blue eyes were most noticeable on his tanned face. He mostly worked in the Emergency Ward. Even though Emergency was always very busy, he had to agree with Ryan that something unusual was going on lately. The increase in accidents and patients presenting over the last three to four months was noticeable. Yesterday included a big four-car accident and a shooting, and on top of the regular patients it was extremely busy and demanding.

Ryan had received a scholarship and was a resident medical officer. He was handsome like Michael with blue eyes and darker blond hair, but if the two of them went out together, the girls usually looked at Michael first. Michael and Ryan had a lot in common through their medical profession and love of sports. Ryan's work and helping humanity would always be Ryan's first priority. They had become very strong friends over the last three months.

Michael had first noticed Ryan when he was speaking to Dr Newell the hospital CEO and had been very impressed with the obvious familiarity between the two. He had thought that maybe it might be beneficial to know someone who was so close to his supervisor. Ryan had explained he knew Dr Newell as the father of his girlfriend Ashley, and also how the two of them were connected through his volunteer work at the Foundation.

Ryan was going to the Newell charity fundraiser tonight and Michael had agreed to attend and learn about the Foundation. Michael had been to many charity events with his mother and was particularly looking forward to this one. There were no expensive tickets to buy; you pledged a donation or volunteered your time at the Foundation or you just came and joined in the fun. They appreciated the funds but apparently the financial side of things always took care of itself and the event always did well. You didn't have to wear a tuxedo and the event was held at Dr Newell's house.

Ryan had said that Dr Newell and his wife Patricia threw the best parties with close to one thousand people expected to attend. The Newell's had family money but were very down to earth people. Dr Newell was also a mentor at the university and his wife was a social worker. The Foundation was their own initiative.

As they headed to the showers after their game, Michael asked, "Are you staying at Doctor Newell's after you have set up this afternoon or going back to your place to change for the event?"

"It'll only take a couple of hours so I'll head back to my place."

"Can I pick you up and we go together?" Michael didn't want to go to the party alone.

"Great," said Ryan, "Is seven OK for you?"

Michael loved driving. Driving to Ryan's house and then the party would really relax him.

* * *

Michael was on time. They drove for about forty minutes with Ryan giving directions. As Michael turned his BMW into the driveway he did not expect to see a property fit for royalty.

"This house has been owned by the Newells for generations," said Ryan. Michael stared in amazement, trying to take in the grand entrance. "I was the same when I first saw this house." Ryan said, smiling. The driveway was long and lined either side by well-maintained trees. The house was a large double storey mansion built from thick red concrete blocks. It looked like a plantation home with a large white entrance of six columns that spanned from the step landing of the first floor up to the roof of the second floor.

As they neared the end of the driveway, a fountain placed perfectly in the center of the lawn spurted water high in the air. "Doctor Newell's private residence is very impressive," said Michael. They stopped at the valet parking and went inside the house. Ryan was already known to the staff so he and Michael were welcomed in. They walked into the west side of the house where the party was being held. It was very crowded.

"I know where Emily and Ashley will be," offered Ryan, who was very familiar with the house plan.

"Thank you, but I think it would be rude not to say hello to Doctor Newell first."

Ryan agreed and they moved through the crowd. Dr Newell thanked them for seeking him out and said it was good to see them. After greetings were exchanged and compliments were made on the decor, Ryan excused himself and Michael stayed to talk with Dr Newell.

"This is a good-sized house to hold such a large fundraiser," said Michael.

"Yes, it's been in the family for many generations. We hold our own annual charity event here and offer the house for many different events throughout the year. Patricia, my wife, loves working with the organizers."

Michael always had conversation ready that was very interesting and entertaining, and the conversation flowed easily. After several minutes Ryan reappeared. "The ladies are requesting your company, Michael." They said their goodbyes to Dr Newell and headed over. As they got closer, Michael leant close to Ryan and said, "Emily is much more beautiful than the photo you showed me." Ryan nodded. Michael said hello to Ashley, who he already knew from the hospital, and then to Emily. As soon the introductions were done, Ryan grabbed Ashley's hand and pulled her away. He clearly wanted to spend some time alone with her. "We're going to get a drink. Michael, Emily, what would you like?"

"I'm driving so I'll have a soda please," replied Michael.

"Nothing for me," said Emily.

* * *

Emily wasn't shy, but she was a little surprised to be left alone straight away with this handsome stranger while her best friends went to get a drink. Michael was taller than Emily and had the same athletic build. Ashley had described him well; he was ruggedly handsome.

"Thank you for coming tonight. Ryan said you may be interested in learning more about the Foundation?" asked Emily.

"I am. I would really like to see how this fundraiser works first. It's so different to the charity events I attend with my mother."

"Please follow me and I'll show you how it all comes together." Michael and Emily walked through the entertaining section of the house before arriving at the educational business section.

Emily showed him the room that was set up with the banquet dinner consisting of seafood, game, meat, exotic dishes and exquisite vegetable platters. No matter your food preferences, they were available in abundant supplies. The room was set up with an assortment of table heights to suit if you wanted to sit or stand.

"The food looks fabulous. Did you fly in an overseas chef?" asked Michael.

"No, never. We only ever source local talent and supplies so the money is used to help our people and our economy. We like to recycle the money." Emily showed Michael the desserts room filled with tables laden with culinary delights. The bar was next and Michael felt like it was from a grand hotel, it was so big and very well stocked. Between the food and the Foundation displays was the band and the dance floor. "While we're on the tour," said Emily, "would you like to dance?"

They had two dances together, but the music wasn't slow enough to embrace. They smiled a lot at each other but conversation was limited to the breaks with the band. At the end of the second dance Emily said, "Thank you. You're a great dancer, but it's back to the tour. The Foundation displays are in this room. We would love you to be interested, but I don't want to pressure you. So have a look around, eat, drink and have an enjoyable time."

"Thank you, Emily, for the tour. I enjoyed our dances and hope we can do it all again soon," replied Michael, walking towards the display room.

* * *

Michael looked at the different displays highlighting the services provided by the Foundation. They offered services for all ages and all categories of assistance. The Newell family managed the Foundation. It was no secret that they used the family's money through the Foundation.

Michael picked up a brochure and read Dr Newell's bio. It was pretty impressive. Dr Newell looked after the scholarship/education portfolio, mentoring the medical students, overseeing the trade school, managing the sheltered workshops and administering the university scholarships. He had a large staff to support him.

Another brochure showed that Patricia worked with the homeless, which was a little different to what he now saw was Emily's youth focus. Patricia assessed for the alcohol detox clinics, shelters for domestic violence, clinics for mental health, the food bank and even offered hospitality classes. Emily liked to enroll the homeless youth into the education classes so they could be eligible for a scholarship. All girls work on the food vans.

This family is truly amazing, thought Michael.

There were fifty silent auctions on display. The prizes had been donated and each one was one Michael would have loved to have bought. The prices were very high, due to the guests' generosity. While he couldn't afford to bid, he did think about volunteering his services.

Michael went to the bar for another soda, then to the banquet hall where he filled a plate. He smiled as he thought of his mother and this beautiful food, the expensive event, and so far, it had not cost him even the price of a ticket. He didn't want to impose on Emily or interrupt Ryan and Ashley, so he decided to further his relationship with Dr Newell which would be even more beneficial now that he had met Emily. Dr Newell had barely moved from his earlier spot. "Hello Doctor Newell, I've met your lovely daughter Emily and visited the Foundation displays. No wonder you're so proud of the Foundation and the good you're responsible for. May I join you again?"

"Yes, we are proud and we do use this money very wisely. I'm glad you have some food, Michael. I was just telling everyone about the influx of emergencies at work. It's rather strange, isn't it?" said Dr Newell. It wasn't long before the conversations were all about the hospital and work. Dr Newell's group of friends appeared familiar with this topic and all had an interest, opinion or comment to add to the conversation.

*   *   *

The food was being eaten, the bar was well visited and the dance floor constantly packed. An hour before midnight, Dr Martin Newell went to the microphone and called for everyone's attention. He welcomed everyone and spoke briefly about the origins and growth of the Foundation. This was an annual event so Martin kept it short for the regulars. Martin called on the Foundation CEO to say some words.

The CEO introduced himself as "Henry" and said that they were well over raising the expected one million dollars and, once again, thank you to Dr Newell and his wife Patricia for funding and hosting the charity event. Henry called on Patricia to say a few words about the planned projects. Patricia was enthusiastic, well-spoken and excited to explain the new projects, the additional services and express the gratitude for everyone's generosity. Patricia especially thanked the volunteers and staff who make it all possible. She could not resist and had to mention Emily and Ashley for their tireless work. Most of the guests were standing, so the applause automatically became a standing ovation.

Michael had not met Patricia yet, but really liked her enthusiasm, honesty and obvious love of her family. Guests were ushered into the dessert hall for coffee and cake, or the bar for final drinks. It was getting late so many guests were catching up with friends to say their goodbyes. Michael went to find Ryan and Ashley. They were alone, enjoying each other's company and so in love. As a warning, Michael coughed loudly as he approached. Ashley and Ryan accepted the warning and stopped kissing long enough to speak with Michael.

"Thank you, Ryan, for arranging this invitation. I'll be looking further into the Foundation. I get what you mean about this family. They're so genuine and make everyone feel welcome. I'm heading home, do you want a lift?"

"Ashley will drive me home. She's staying at my place tonight," said Ryan. "Thank you for the offer. I'll see you soon."

Michael said his goodbyes to both of them and went to find Emily. "This fundraiser was really fun. Thank you for our tour and dances and I hope I see you again soon."

"Thank you, Michael. Are you leaving now?"

"As soon as I say goodbye to your father. Goodnight, Emily." Michael found Dr. Newell, shook his hand again and said his courtesy goodbye, thanking him for his company and conversation throughout the evening. Dr Newell thanked Michael in return. Before Michael could leave, Dr Newell's wife joined them.

"Hello, my name is Patricia. I'm Doctor Newell's wife and Emily's mother. I know your name is Michael. I noticed you and Martin have had an interesting night with plenty of laughs."

Michael was taken aback, but skilled enough to hide his shock. He had noticed this extremely wealthy woman didn't dress like his own status-conscious mother. But standing before him was Patricia addressing him in such a friendly manner. *My parents will definitely not cope with these people*, thought Michael. He had seen Patricia throughout the evening and marveled that this woman always had a circle of people around her and how everyone enjoyed her company. He instantly loved Patricia as she was friendly, accepting and bubbly. She made Michael feel as though she was genuinely happy to have met him.

"Yes," said Michael, "I've enjoyed tonight's great company. Thank you, Patricia, it was lovely to meet you and your family." He wished he had of been close enough to have hugged her without it being awkward.

Michael said his goodbyes again and made his way back to the front door. *I'll contact Ryan tomorrow, and have Ryan ask Ashley to set up a double date with Emily*, thought Michael as he walked through the front door. Michael turned around to look back inside the house. Without the big crowd, he could see the painted walls and decorative finishes. He admired the expensive house again, closed the front door and walked down the stairs and over to the valet parking. He handed over his key tag and waited for the valet to drive his car to him. He drove slowly around the other side of the circular driveway. While this had been the best fundraiser Michael had ever attended and he had felt so welcomed, he realized he needed to relax around his mother and just enjoy life.

He could not stop thinking, *I've had a great night with Dr Newell. I really like Emily and Patricia and I don't think I can wipe this big smile off my face.* He enjoyed that he could still see the lit-up house in his rear-view mirror as he drove down the driveway. This night has worked out better than expected.

Chapter Three

It had taken Ryan and Ashley a whole two weeks after the fundraiser to set up a date with Emily and Michael. Emily was very independent and sometimes didn't give a guy much of a chance so she hadn't been overly keen.

Her father couldn't stop talking about Michael's ability with the latest demands in Emergency. He thought Michael was a natural leader and planned to mentor him for development. Emily didn't have time to form her own judgment on the handsome doctor. Everyone seemed to like Michael. The expectation was a silent burden to Emily.

Emily was taking her time getting dressed in front of the tall standalone mirror. She didn't know what to wear for a date with a near stranger. Ashley, clearly tired of the wardrobe changes, sighed and rolled her eyes. "Argh, enough changes. You look fine."

Emily ignored her friend's tone as she had done many times before. They were best friends, more like sisters, with a long history between them. Emily settled on a dress alleviating Ashley's impatience.

"I'll wait for you downstairs while you apply your makeup. I'm going to get a drink," said Ashley. She turned to face Emily on her way out. "Em, you look great. I'm sure Michael is just happy to be meeting up with you."

"Thanks Ash, I'll meet you down stairs." Emily sat at the makeup vanity which was her grandmother's. When her grandmother had turned twenty-one, she had received the makeup vanity from her parents and, in turn, had given it to Emily for her twenty-first birthday, now lovingly restored and maintaining its antique elegance in memory. Emily and Ashley loved every piece of furniture in this room as it told a story and formed the jigsaw of their lives. Emily, especially, felt it was a time capsule of memories with a timeless charm.

When she'd finished, Emily entered the walk-in and turned on the light. The large room was filled with shelving and only a few pairs of shoes. Even though the walk-in was big enough to be a small shoe store, it was only partially filled. Emily would never over indulge for herself with so many homeless people on the streets in need of food and shelter. She could not justify spending money recklessly on luxury items.

Emily stood near the small selection of shoes, looked at each pair and thought, *At least Michael is tall, so I don't have to worry about the heel.* Finally dressed, Emily walked over and closed the French doors to the front balcony. She never bothered to pull the drapes as her bedroom was set back from the balcony and the house was a good distance from the street. *I don't know what's more exciting, that I'm going out on a date or that I'm going out with Michael,* Emily thought. Emily hadn't been on a double date since Robert, and that was over nine months ago. Robert had been great. His only real fault was all he really wanted was children. A sense of anxiety consumed her, the pressure of the date returning. *I'm sure Dad will still mentor Michael even if this date doesn't work out,* she thought. But she wasn't really sure.

Emily knew if she wasn't on time, her father would take the time to speak to Michael and Ryan about the influx of cases to

Emergency and would use this topic as a lead in to talk work. Emily didn't want to share her date and knew the onus was on her and Ashley for an on-time departure. Emily made her way downstairs with fifteen minutes to spare before the men were due to arrive. Her parents and Ashley were in the kitchen. "Dad, please don't get into a conversation with Michael and Ryan. Ashley has a movie to watch at nine."

He smiled a knowing smile. "Now, what would make you think I'd delay your date?"

Patricia laughed. "Sweetheart, just go and enjoy yourself. Your father has only positive things to say about Michael. We'll say hello only, so don't worry. I'll hold your father back."

Emily reminded her parents that she would be spending the night at her city apartment and Ashley was sleeping at Ryan's. The doorbell rang and, surprisingly, Emily had to stop herself from running. The four friends greeted each other in the foyer. Michael's excitement was obvious, his eyes glowing as he looked at Emily.

"I see you all have the night off. Have a wonderful evening and please look after my girls," joked Martin. He winked at Emily, as if to say, "That's it, I haven't trapped them."

Everyone said their farewells and Patricia and Martin followed them out. Michael held the car door open and Emily was impressed. She knew her parents would have been impressed too. As she wound down the car window, she could hear them reminiscing.

"Remember when we went on our first date?" said Patricia.

"Like it was yesterday," he replied. They smiled at each other, turned and then walked back to the kitchen.

Emily directed Michael to Manhattan even though she noticed he could have used his GPS. Ryan had booked the restaurant near the fountain. He'd heard great reviews and decided it was time for Ashley and Emily to try this one. The friends usually took it in turns to select different venues. Emily knew her friends didn't expect nor want her to pay their meal bill, so they always picked reasonably priced venues so everyone could enjoy the evening and easily split the tab.

The double date would be cut short after dinner so Ashley and Ryan could leave to watch a movie at nine, leaving Emily and Michael on their own. There was unlikely to be parking outside the restaurant but Michael drove past anyway. Finding parking in New York City was only by chance. Cars perfectly lined up along the sidewalk, so close a person wouldn't be able to walk in between them.

"Sorry everyone, but we have no chance of finding parking here. I hope you don't mind a walk," said Michael.

"Not at all, it's to be expected," replied Emily.

"No problem. It's a lovely evening anyway," said Ashley.

Michael found parking two blocks north of the restaurant. Emily and Michael walked in front of Ashley and Ryan. Each couple held their own conversation, occasionally talking backwards or forward to the other couple. As the group walked past two homeless men, Michael took Emily's hand which caused a flutter to beat through her heart. She was surprised that she was so excited to be on a date with Michael.

Michael held the door open with a warm expression as Emily walked past first, then Ashley and Ryan followed through the opened door. Ryan confirmed the booking and reached for Ashley's hand. The group was escorted to a table at the back of the small restaurant, positioned quietly in the corner. It had a double-window view of the Bethesda Fountain. The restaurant was fully occupied as it was summer and was popular with locals and tourists.

Michael was looking through the front window of the restaurant. "That homeless man must be hungry to just be standing there."

"If he's standing there, he must be hungry," commented Emily without turning. "The homeless are not usually so obvious." Emily gestured for the waiter. "May I please place a separate takeout order for now? I'll pay for it straightaway and then we'll order our meals to have here."

Ryan had seen this same scene many times, but it was all new to Michael. Ashley had been at the bathroom and sat down without noticing the man at the window. Michael stared affectionately at Emily; he smiled softly. The waiter bought the bill for the takeout order.

"Emily is very committed to helping the people on the street. It's something her mother is also passionate about," said Ryan. "The Newells are always supportive of those less fortunate."

Emily smiled and paid the bill. The man seemed familiar to her, but she couldn't remember where she'd seen him before. The homeless man was staring at her strangely. "I wonder why he's standing there?" remarked Emily, more as an observation than a judgment.

"Maybe he's seen you in a restaurant before and he knows something from the kitchen is headed his way," said Ryan.

"Buying meals is very generous," stated Michael, amazed. "There are not many families that share their success with those less fortunate."

"Ashley and I work with so many different people and the one thing in common is they are grateful to receive food. I hope the two men are still outside when the food is ready. Otherwise, I'll just leave it on the seat for them later," said Emily.

"Are you going out to tell them some food is coming?" asked Michael

"No. I've learnt the correct protocol with food. If I hand it to them and say nothing, that's acceptable. If I ask them to wait for the food I've just ordered, that's not acceptable and they'll leave."

The baffled waiter gave the bag to Emily. "This is most unusual. Enjoy the meal!" He looked very confused.

"Thank you," said Emily. The man was still watching. Emily stood up to take the food out. Michael stopped her.

"Please let me take it out. The man at the window seems to be infatuated with you. I would feel safer if I went out and handed them the food."

Emily didn't feel unsafe, but didn't want to argue or make the event bigger than it need be, so she agreed.

* * *

A group of four headed into a restaurant behind where John sat with Roger on the sidewalk. John recognized two of the group as the ladies from the accident scene a couple of weeks ago. *There's that strange woman again,* he thought, staring at Emily.

"Do you think we'll get some food tonight?" asked Roger.

John ignored the question. Roger was truly homeless, not like him, and always looking for food. They only met at night. For some reason, John had grown fond of Roger. He didn't make it a practice to spend time or get attached to people from this place. Besides, John had other things to worry about right now other than food. He went to the restaurant window to get a closer look at the group.

"What are you doing?" asked Roger from the sidewalk.

"Just looking." John stared in the window. *It's impossible,* he thought. He knew they were all watching him, but it didn't matter. John needed to find out who Emily was. He didn't understand at all. The waiter had taken a bag of takeout food to the table, and now a man from the group walked through the door towards him.

"My lady friend has bought you both some food. Did you want to take it over to your friend so you can eat it while it's still hot?" asked Michael.

John took the food, mumbled "Thanks" and went to his friend. As they enjoyed the meal, John looked back wondering, *Why has she bought us this food? It wasn't what most people do. Was she just trying to remove me from the window or did she understand that I'm hungry?*

John determined that the group had interpreted his presence as hunger which was good because he didn't want to be obvious while he was working things out. He would have to monitor this situation for an answer. And that woman, Emily …*Who was she?*

* * *

Michael sat back down across from Emily. "The man said thanks. Hey, the smell of food has made me hungry. Let's order." They all reached for their menus. Michael ordered last, adding a bottle of wine. After the wine had been shared by the four friends, they all ordered nonalcoholic drinks. Medicine and fitness ensured a sober night.

As they ate their meals, the conversation flowed easily about the hospital. Michael, Ashley and Ryan were working there and Emily had heard all about it from her father. Over the last three to four months, the number of street deaths had declined but presentations to Emergency had increased. It was having an impact on all the staff. Ambulance and hospital staff were overworked and police didn't have a reason why.

The evening ticked by so quickly and easily. The movie session was starting soon so Ryan and Ashley finished their meals, gave Michael some money for the bill and said their goodbyes. Emily and Michael watched them leave, turned and looked at each other and smiled. Their date had started. Luckily, the awkwardness was gone.

"Michael, what made you choose medicine as your career?"

"When I was a child my cat got run over and I was unhappy not knowing how to help it. I've studied at Yale and the rest is history."

Emily believed she could sense the pureness of people. She looked at it as a strange sort of gift that other people didn't have. She didn't understand it but always went with her feelings. She had chosen psychology as her course of study because of it. She felt compelled to help those in need and assist them in making the right life choices.

Emily felt Michael was a good person. She sensed he wasn't as good a person as Ryan, but he wasn't a bad person either. But she had this strange unease she couldn't quite put her finger on. "Michael, why did you come to the charity event? Was it to learn about the Foundation?"

"Do I need a motive?" replied Michael. "Ryan told me about the event and I was really interested to compare it to my mother's events. Now, to be honest, I'm glad to be sitting here with you all to myself."

"So how did the events differ?" asked Emily.

Michael explained how his mother's events were all about the clothes, jewelry and status; very little was about the actual charity. To attend the Foundation event and have such a wonderful time was very refreshing for him. He could not believe the focus wasn't on the clothes and the fashion, and that the event had raised so much money.

Emily explained how she usually never wore expensive dresses, but the dress she wore on that night had been a collaboration between Ashley and Patricia. They had bought it because Emily had already worn the same dress three times to the annual events and would have worn it a fourth time if they had not intervened. Ashley designed the new dress which was very understated but ridiculously expensive. Emily finished with a laugh, "Mom said I'll wear it so many times, it will pay for itself."

"It was a lovely dress and you did look beautiful," replied Michael.

"Good compliment!" exclaimed Emily, starting to realize why her friends thought the two were suited. "So, tell me about your family. And, who is Michael?" Emily wasn't able to take her eyes off his handsome face.

"My father is an investment banker on Wall Street and my mother is my mother. Let's say she's not as generous or kind as you are towards such things as homeless people. Status is very important to my parents. My younger brother Samuel is a Harvard lawyer with a girlfriend who is always in magazines and on TV," said Michael. "In answer to your question about me, I've worked really hard in medicine and I'm truly proud of where I am and the impact I have and will have in the future due to my knowledge and my skills. I'm a dedicated doctor. OK," said Michael. "Let's lighten the mood. Tell me about your family and who Emily is."

There was a moment's silence as Emily thought about what she would tell Michael about herself. She owed Michael the same level of honesty but didn't usually let someone in so early in a relationship. She ignored her usual judgment. "My parents are the most generous people in the world," said Emily. "I don't just mean with money, but with everything. They decided when they first got married that they wouldn't have children to indulge or detract from their work. They would help all the children of the world. As it happened, their circumstances … changed and I was adopted. They have given me the gifts of humanity and we're so proud of each other. I am who I am because of them, and they say they are who they are because of me. I know this sounds really corny, but a relationship with me is a package deal. You get me and my parents."

"I know your father a little bit through work, I've met your mother and find her refreshing and I've really enjoyed my time now with you. I hope you're considering me for the package deal?"

"When we first met, you mentioned you were interested in my humanitarian work. I spend a lot of time with lost youth during the day and the homeless people at night. If you ever want to help, we can always use an extra pair of hands. Especially doctor hands or even sport training? You saw the list of Foundation departments and services?"

"I'll make the time. Just let me know when." They talked easily about their love of sport and the many games they had in common. "Do you play golf?" asked Michael.

"Dad has taken me a couple of times. My average is ninety for eighteen. Dad thinks I have a hidden talent. But then again, no matter what I do, Dad thinks it's a hidden talent."

"Well, I need to see this! I have mornings free next week. How about next Friday?"

"I'll check my schedule, but I'm usually free on Fridays."

"You and Ashley seem to be really close; you have common career goals and I think you even look like sisters. When did you meet?" asked Michael.

Emily sat back and smiled. She always enjoyed talking about her friendship with Ashley.

Chapter Four

Emily told Michael the whole story.

Ashley's father had been murdered by a man who'd chosen a life of drugs. He'd been at the wrong place at the wrong time. The drug addict didn't even remember the murder and therefore didn't display remorse. Ashley was an only child and had been adored by her father. Jan, her mother, was unwittingly selfish in her grieving, thinking that a five-year-old didn't need comfort and support like an adult. Jan thought the loss of love and income only affected her as the surviving parent, so Ashley suffered on her own, knowing that her mother wouldn't be capable of providing the same unconditional love as her father.

By the age of seven, the local school had identified, tested and recommended that Ashley attend a school that offered a Talented and Gifted program (TAG). Ashley was highly intelligent for her age and needed an education that would develop her gift.

Jan was already working two jobs and knew she wouldn't be able to pay the fees for a prestigious school. The local school suggested a scholarship program and recommended a boarding school in Manhattan, New York. Jan agreed to let Ashley sit the scholarship exam, and she was awarded the Newell Scholarship, and started school when she was eight years old.

Ashley struggled when she found that she was no longer the popular girl, but the poor girl on a free ride. This school was full of status-conscience families and Ashley felt lost. This was when Emily first met Ashley; they were both eight years old and Emily was also a part-time border at the school. Emily met Ashley in TAG classes. Emily was impressed with Ashley's intelligence and knew there had been a lot of pain in her short life.

Emily and Ashley found they had a lot of sports interests. Ashley wanted to be a doctor to help people and Emily wanted to be a psychologist, so an immediate friendship formed. Ashley was made to feel like an accepted friend regardless of status. Emily had had no idea Ashley was on the Newell Scholarship, but once she found out she was so proud that such a worthy person like Ashley had been awarded the chance. Both girls were dedicated to their education and both enjoyed their fun times together.

After a couple of months, Emily spoke to her parents about her best friend and explained how they really missed each other on the weekends. Emily loved coming home and always did wonderful things on the weekend. Emily would return to school on the Monday to find Ashley had been very lonely as she was shunned by staff and students.

The Newell's wanted to help Emily's friend. The scholarship funding was increased to cover casual clothes, provide a small living allowance and cover the costs for Ashley to fly home to visit her mom during term break. With Jan's permission, Ashley could also accompany Emily home on the school weekends. Ashley was welcomed into the Newell family and their lovely home.

Ashley's mother eventually remarried and had more children, and under Jan's advice Ashley didn't fly home each school break. Emily and Ashley were now like sisters. When Ashley was ten, the Newell's asked Jan if Ashley could be removed from the scholarship program and placed under their supervision. The Newells loved Ashley and Ashley loved them. Emily felt she had a sister and Martin and Pat felt they now had two loving and generous twin daughters.

Emily and Ashley graduated from school and attended the same college and medical school. The girls appreciated the opportunities they had been given and as they were very studious, they were not interested in the educational party scene. Now aged twenty-five, they are completing their residency and working at the Foundation for a casual wage. They would prefer to volunteer for free, but Patricia insists they'll have plenty of time in the future to volunteer without the many bills of today.

"And that," said Emily, "is how we became the best of friends."

* * *

Emily and Michael had been laughing and enjoying an easy conversation which halted when Michael's phone rang. "It's Ryan." said Michael. Emily could only hear the one-way conversation.

"Emily and I are still at the restaurant and we were thinking of walking to the fountain. Would you and Ashley like to meet us there?" asked Michael. After a small chuckle he continued, "Great! See you there." Michael disconnected the call and smiled at Emily. "I forgot all about them."

"Me too, and Ashley is my best friend! The time has passed so quickly… and enjoyably."

Michael gestured for the waiter. "We're ready for the check please."

"Michael, if it's not too much trouble, would you be able to drop me at my apartment, rather than my parents' home? It's in the Upper East Side, only five minutes from the restaurant. Ashley is staying at Ryan's tonight so you'll still have great company on the drive."

"I was hoping to chat some more during the drive back to Scarsdale, but it's no problem at all to drive you wherever you need to go." The waiter returned with the small leather folder and handed it to Michael. Emily reached for her purse gesturing for that she wanted to share the bill, but Michael insisted.

"Please Emily, let me pay for our first date. It will be the last time I insist on paying the whole bill." Emily agreed, as she didn't want to make a scene over the check. She also didn't believe him. The waiter walked away and Michael thanked Emily for a perfect first date. He slipped the bill into the folder and then they left the restaurant.

Michael and Emily held hands as they crossed over to the fountain; it was spectacular at night. Conversation flowed as they walked past one of the homeless men, alone with the takeaway bag beside him, now half full. As they approached the fountain and away from the man, Michael pulled Emily in for a kiss. The kiss was soft and cautionary.

Emily responded, her lips moving in sequence with his. This was the best kiss she'd ever had. Michael was obviously well practiced and moved his whole mouth in a very sensual way. At that moment, Emily was very connected to Michael, enjoying the passion, the tenderness, the skill and the excitement. Michael's hands rested lightly on her face. He was very confident to let his sensual kiss set the mood. It was very sexual to not have a man's hands and body moving and detracting from the desire. For some strange reason, Emily started to think about her father wondering if this kiss was Michael's way of trying to get closer to Dr. Newell through a relationship with her.

She cleared her mind and refocused on the kiss. They both pulled away and smiled.

"Perfect!" exclaimed Michael.

Emily blushed. "To say the least." Emily returned for a second kiss and could feel Michael smile as her lips met his.

It was a shorter version of the first kiss as they were suddenly parted by the sound of Ryan's voice.

"I don't think we need to ask you how your date was." Ashley laughed as they all walked back to the car.

"Horribly," laughed Emily.

"We were spied on," joked Michael.

"We've had a good night," said Emily. "How was the movie?

"I don't think Ryan saw any of it, but he did laugh when he saw me cry," said Ashley.

"You know I only go to watch you next to me," said Ryan lovingly.

The laughter was coming to an end as they approached the car. Michael led Emily around to the back of the car while Ryan and Ashley made their way into the back seat.

"We only have a short drive to your city apartment and as I'll be dropping you off first, do you mind if I kiss you before you get in the car rather than at your place in front of our car audience?" whispered Michael.

Emily nodded and then felt excited at the prospect of another Michael kiss. Neither rushed the kiss and neither stopped at one. When they parted some minutes later, Michael helped Emily into her passenger seat, shutting the door softly behind her.

"I don't know, Ryan, do you think their date was a success? Do we know our friends?" Ashley asked.

"Ash are you still staying at Ryan's tonight?" asked Emily as Michael pulled into the front of the apartment building.

"Yes. I'll see you tomorrow."

"Thank you all for a great night, Michael. Bye Ryan. Ash, see you tomorrow then."

Emily reached her apartment, opening the door and only concentrating on the ecstasy of the events that night. Michael had at least a forty-minute drive to Ryan's house. She reached into her bag to get her phone so she could start texting Ashley about the date. Without having to ask, Ashley would be mentally taking notes of Michael's revelations on the way home.

Oh no, where is it? Calm down, when did you see it last? thought Emily. She remembered it in her bag when she reached for her wallet to pay for the takeout.

Emily used the home phone and rang the restaurant. They had found her phone on the floor. They would be leaving in half an hour. If she couldn't make it back by then, they would hold the phone until Monday. Emily could not live without her phone for one hour, let alone forty-eight. She rushed to the garage and jumped into her car. Emily had started the car's engine and was driving out of the garage zipping towards the restaurant in less than a minute.

Chapter Five

It was now late at night so Emily was able to park very close to the restaurant. She walked quickly to the restaurant to collect her phone, but as Emily returned to her car, she was preoccupied with getting her phone back and so wasn't taking her usual precautions when she was approached by a man. Emily could feel he was pure evil. She tried to keep walking even though something in her mind told her to run.

The man pulled a large knife from his pocket. Emily looked at the man, the knife and then looked around to see if anyone could help her. She was alone and vulnerable. She stood motionless and let the man control the situation. Oddly, she didn't fear the outcome. That same weird flutter trembled though Emily's heart. It was different to before, and she sensed it was a result of fear. She saw the homeless man in the distance and called out to him.

As soon as the knife-wielding man saw the homeless man, he acted like he had something to prove. Emily had become just a pawn in a game where she didn't know the rules. The evil man lunged. Emily instinctively tried to block but it was too late, it was all happened so quick. The knife slashed deep into Emily's arm. He dragged it across her skin, creating a deeper wound.

Stunned and in absolute shock, Emily could not believe that she could be attacked so savagely by a random man in such an innocent situation. No sooner than this thought had passed through her mind, the man clutched at his heart as though having a heart attack. Emily looked at her arm, expecting to see bone as the cut was so deep. But her arm wasn't bleeding, there was not cut and no pain. The evil man stared at Emily, then at his own arm. Blood was streaming from his arm – not from a deep cut, but from a surface gash that required stitches rather than surgery. The blood-covered knife was on the floor and the man dropped to the floor in pain to join it.

"What did you do?" The man yelled at the homeless man. "My boss warned me about you. Who are you?"

Emily had forgotten about the homeless man until now. She was unable to talk, unable to move. She scanned her memory for answers. Had she accidently gotten hold of the knife and pushed back? Was the robber's intention to self-harm? Did the homeless man intercept the attack?

"Leave now and go home," the homeless man shouted.

Emily picked up her bag and phone from the ground and ran to her car. The voice had sounded familiar, but she wasn't going to hang around any longer. She was in an unfamiliar place, it was late, something unexplainable had happened, someone was hurt and yet she knew she could leave the homeless man and he would be OK.

On the short drive back to her apartment, with all her car doors locked, Emily could not understand what had just happened. She felt the homeless man was involved, yet he'd only watched from a distance. What did the attacker know about the homeless man? Who was the attacker's boss? Replaying the scenario, Emily knew the homeless man had come to protect her. The sense of fear was replaced with relief, even though he wasn't physically doing anything. He'd just watched. Had he intervened? Did he quickly cover the distance to assist with the attack? But how?

So many questions with no answers. Emily knew a long restless night was before her as she replayed the scenario over and over again in her mind. As she approached her garage, a text message arrived, but she was too distracted to read it.

Chapter Six

Emily had a very restless night. She still felt shocked from the random attack and had stayed awake tossing and turning, trying to work out what had happened. She was wide awake staring at the ceiling long before the warm morning sunrays shone through her bedroom windows.

Emily stretched her legs and arms, and let out a loud yawn. Clearly today wasn't going to be very productive. Emily loved this apartment; it was a simple two-bedroom unit, with the main bedroom belonging to Ashley as she primarily occupied the apartment. It had a decent sized office which they shared. Most of the windows overlooked Central Park.

Emily lay in the safety of her bed and looked around her room. The bedroom door was closed which was unusual. Maybe it was because she was alone in the apartment, that she had felt so vulnerable last night. She was in no hurry to start her day. Ashley was expected back at ten. She could do with having a conversation that would help her put together the events of the previous night. Emily pulled up her sleeve and stared at the perfectly unharmed forearm. By all accounts it should have needed stitching, been wrapped in bandages, maybe even hospitalization. Emily ran her hand down her unblemished arm still confused about the events of the night before.

Emily picked up her phone and saw messages from Michael and Ashley. She opened Michael's first and with a smile began to read. "Thank you for the wonderful night. I had fun and can't wait to do it all again." The delight in knowing Michael enjoyed the night lifted her mood.

She messaged back, "Me too. I look forward to meeting up again soon." Ashley had messaged three times, clearly eager to talk. Emily didn't return any messages and decided to get out of bed. She wouldn't return to sleep. The loneliness of the morning left her mind thinking that today could have been much worse.

Emily stepped into the shower and stood motionless under the warm water, washing away the stress of the night. It wasn't until five minutes later that she reached for the shampoo and began to wash her hair. Emily didn't want this to consume her, she wanted to find answers and move on. She had already laid her clothes out for the day. They were casual, matching her mood.

Emily continued analyzing as she ate her cereal. She had turned on the TV hoping to hear a news report about last night's event. Ashley's key unlocking the door so she switched the TV off.

"Sorry I didn't text last night. I can explain, I think," said Emily.

Ashley walked into the kitchen and retrieved a bottle of water. "Good. I really expected to be chatting with you rather than listening to Ryan and Michael on the drive home."

"I know. Sorry. OK, where do I begin?"

* * *

"Michael was great, we're going to meet up again. I need your help with something else," Emily said.

Ashley had sat down next to Emily and had been expecting the conversation to lead straight into Michael, including details of what had happened at the restaurant and about that fountain kiss.

"After Michael dropped me home, I had to return to the restaurant to retrieve my phone. While walking back to the car I was attacked," said Emily.

Ashley gasped. "What! Oh my goodness! Are you alright?"

"I'm OK, though still a little confused. I was in shock last night and didn't want to upset you as well."

"I would have come straight back to spend the night with you. What happened?"

"I've replayed the whole thing over and over in my mind and it still doesn't make sense. I'll tell you and then will you come back to the restaurant with me for some sort of verification?" asked Emily.

"Of course, but you're starting to scare me. What happened?"

"When I walked out of the restaurant, I was really happy to have my phone back. Then a man came up to me and just slashed a knife at my arm," said Emily, baring her arm and holding it out for Ashley to see.

Ashley was now skeptical about the event. The realness in Emily's tone compared to the lack of evidence confused her. She cautioned her responses, not wanting to sound unsupportive. "Um, OK? I don't see anything. Do you see something?"

Emily pulled her arm away. "That's the problem. The attacker fell to the ground with the knife cut on his own arm. I don't know how or why it happened. I got to my car as quickly as I could. I didn't call as I really needed to just calm down. What would I have said? I was attacked but not attacked? What could you have done?"

"Why are we going back to the restaurant...?" asked Ashley.

"I don't know. I don't know what I expect to see, but I need to try and gain some clarity. I'm feeling so confused. I can't pretend that it didn't happen."

"I'll drive and then afterwards we can get some coffee." They walked to the lift and silently watched the numbers light up advising its whereabouts. "This is not the news I was expecting. 'Michael is so lovely, Ashley. He's so funny, Ashley. I can't wait to see if he calls, Ashley,' is what I expected."

"Tell me about it," said Emily. "If it helps "Michael is so lovely, ASHLEY. He's so funny, ASHLEY. He sent me a message last night, ASHLEY." Both girls laughed. "I had a great night with Michael and then this event had to ruin the excitement."

"Did you call him?" asked Ashley.

"If I can't explain it to you, what hope would I have with Michael? It would have undone whatever he thought about me."

"I'm just glad you're OK." They drove for a while in silence. Ashley was able to park very close to the restaurant. Not knowing what to expect, they walked slowly in the direction of the restaurant. Ashley was nervous; the puzzle of Emily's story left her thinking that someone may be watching. Emily didn't go into too much detail so Ashley didn't know what to look for and felt worried not knowing if the mystery assailant would be there or watching.

* * *

There wasn't any blood on the sidewalk. Emily took a deep breath, and shook her head. "There isn't any blood anywhere, so no crime scene." Her heart fluttered, though much softer than last night during the attack. She looked up and her eyes went to the two homeless men sitting on the fountain. One of them was the familiar looking one that had been staring at her through the restaurant window last night. Now she thought about it, he looked like the man that had been there during the attack! She nudged Ashley to look.

"That's John!" said Ashley. "He was the man helping me at the car accident. I remember how handsome he is."

Emily walked over to the two men. She wanted to speak to the homeless man and find out if he knew what happened. "Hello, John. How are you?"

"Hello again," said John. "This is Roger." Roger nodded.

"My name is Emily. John, you were here last night. Can you explain what happened to me?"

"I don't know how to answer that question," replied John.

"Did you see my arm get slashed by that man with the knife?"

"Is it slashed? asked John.

"No," said Emily.

"I saw an evil man choose his own consequence. You had no blood and were not injured."

Emily looked down again at her uninjured arm and then back up at John.

"Did you feel unsafe at any time?" asked John.

"No, and that only added to my confusion. You stood there just staring at me."

"I really don't have an answer for you." John got up and began walking away.

Emily wasn't satisfied with John's response. He was definitely hiding something. "Thank you," said Emily, more to Roger than John. She returned to where Ashley was waiting.

"Ash, I don't get it, there is nothing here to validate what happened. I'm not upset. I'm probably relieved. I'm not hurt and while standing here, I remember I didn't really feel unsafe at any time. More shock than anything. I think I'll have to forget about what happened and put it down to a dream. Come on bodyguard let's grab a coffee."

"Bodyguard?"

"Oh come on, look at you," said Emily, as she purposely and with exaggerated motions swayed her head as though checking for danger. They both laughed.

"Em, you didn't even know what happened last night. This maniac could be anywhere."

"Thank you for coming with me. It's time for coffee and to discuss Michael." The girls looked at each other and both understood there was nothing else for them to say on this matter.

"I know where we can get coffee. Let's head this way," said Ashley leading Emily away from the restaurant. They walked in the direction of the parked car. Both girls fell into their familiar walk, comfortable to be supporting each other. Conversation was all about Michael. In a further five minutes they came to the café.

The girls spent an hour in the café eating, laughing and catching up. Emily soon felt so much better and relaxed. Ashley was always the best medicine, no matter what the problem. After what had turned out to be a long day, they returned to their apartment. Emily decided that a night at Scarsdale would be comforting.

"Ash would you like to come to Scarsdale for dinner?" enquired Emily.

Ashley rarely declined an offer but explained how she was feeling exhausted after a late night with Ryan then a day spent searching for answers about a crime scene that didn't exist. "Em, after this weekend I'll have to say no. Please tell Martin and Pat I say hi."

"Sorry to keep you out so long," said Emily.

"Don't be silly, I had a fantastic day with you. I love our city get-togethers, as weird as they can be."

Chapter Seven

It was a long drive back to the Newell home, and Emily thought about the events of the weekend, Michael and their first kiss, and John and the attack. By the time Emily arrived at the Newell home, she felt peaceful and unruffled.

"Hi Mom and Dad," she called as she entered the house.

"In the kitchen," said Patricia. Emily's parents were preparing the evening dinner.

"Yum ... something smells good," said Emily.

"Ashley rang to say she wouldn't be here for tea," said Patricia. "Well?" asked her mom, who was joined by her dad. "How did the date go? No phone calls and we've had to wait a whole day to find out," said Patricia.

Emily blushed like a high school girl. "Well, so far, Michael is really great. We have so much in common. I know I didn't call you but I've also not called him. Ash and I had a great day. Mom, Dad, if you don't mind I'm a bit tired. I'll just freshen up, call Michael and then we can talk over dinner."

"Off you go. We'll talk later," said Martin Newell.

Emily smiled, turned and walked out of the kitchen. Out of sight, she ran up the stairs to her bedroom. She laughed at her school girl antics and pulled her phone out of her bag. She texted

Michael to thank him for last night and remind him about Friday. Emily then freshened up and went back downstairs. She was starting to relax. Emily helped her parents finish making dinner, served up and sat down at the table.

"So," said Martin, smiling. "Can we guess that Michael has placed a spell on you?"

"Oh Dad, a little." She laughed. "He's so easy to talk to. The night just flew past." Turning to look at Patricia, Emily said, "Mom you know he even hinted that he would be willing to help us with the Foundation."

"Wow, that's great! Looks like the fabulous Michael is fabulous after all," Patricia replied.

Dinner conversation continued with Emily discussing all the sport she had in common with Michael, the planned golf date and Michael's talk to help with the Foundation.

"Well, Michael's ears must be burning right about now but, on a different topic, is Chadi available for Friday?" asked Emily.

"He's all yours," said Martin. "Just let him know the details."

Emily rose from the table and asked if she could be excused from the washing up as she was so tired.

"Emily, there are only three of us, so not much to do. Nice that everything worked out for you last night. Have a good sleep," said Patricia walking over to kiss Emily on the cheek.

"Goodnight, Emily," said Martin, still sitting at the table sipping his cup of tea.

"Thank you. Love you both so much. Goodnight." Emily walked up the stairs to her room. She peeled her clothes off and crawled into bed. She would have loved a relaxing bath, but she felt so tired she needed her bed more.

* * *

When Emily woke she decided to return to the restaurant without Ashley. She had been able to sleep properly and now wanted to try one more time for an explanation of the arm slash event. *I cannot believe I even have a name for the event!* Emily smiled to herself. It was Monday and the restaurant was open. There were a lot of people moving about and Emily had to look very hard for John and Roger. Emily could only see Roger. She bought a sandwich and took it over.

"Roger," called Emily on her approach. She didn't want to scare him and have him run away. "This is for you." Emily handed Roger the sandwich. "Is John around?"

"No, but thank you for the sandwich."

Emily sat next to Roger on the fountain wall. "Will he be coming back here?"

"No, I think he's gone again and won't be back for a while."

"Does he go away a lot?" asked Emily.

"Someone like him will come and go, and then another one will come. I don't know if you will see John again." Roger was eating and enjoying the sandwich.

"What do you mean like him?"

"He can stop evil. I know bad people don't hurt good people when he's watching."

"Would you like another sandwich?" asked Emily.

"Yes, please. Can I have a drink too?"

Emily walked back to the shops, trying to collect her thoughts. Things didn't make sense. She bought two sandwiches and two drinks. "Here you go, Roger," said Emily handing him the food and drinks.

Roger took them, but seemed far away deep in thought. "He was my favorite. He was different to the others. He started out like them but then he changed when there was a big car accident. I don't know … maybe he got hit."

"Thank you for our talk," Emily said, turning to walk away.

"You're not bad, but he became aware of you," concluded Roger.

Emily stared at him blankly. She was more confused than when she had started. Emily knew from her experience at the Foundation that the homeless could sometimes speak in riddles, but something was telling her there was a truth to what Roger was saying.

Chapter Eight

A week before the car accident

The two men stood in front of the cars while their drivers sat inside. They all eyed each other warily, occasionally taking a look at the two briefcases sitting on the ground beside the standing men. The men were dressed expensively, but casually. Both had on sunglasses and one had a hat.

"Know that scrawny kid over there?" asked Joseph.

"Nah. Thought he was with you."

When they looked again, he was gone. Joseph motioned the driver to go take a look, but before the driver could get out of the car, the kid had come out of nowhere, grabbed one of the briefcases and bolted.

Must be getting old, thought Joseph. "Get him!" he yelled to his driver. The two men fumbled for their guns, turned and took aim, but they were too slow. The kid had disappeared. The drivers waited for their bosses to get into the cars and then went in different directions looking for him.

Joseph wasn't happy his briefcase had been stolen. "You need to find that kid, boys."

Making an example was very important. Did he know who he was dealing with?

The day of the accident

"There he is!" shouted Joseph and took chase. He was expensively and not practically dressed, and so wasn't prepared for this street chase. It had taken his boys weeks to find him. But here he was. Joseph kept his eye on his target, noting that he didn't have his briefcase with him. There had been a four-car accident and people were everywhere. It was getting hard to see where the brat was going.

He had to catch that kid!

The chase lasted for four blocks until Joseph's driver cut him off. Joseph soon caught up and pushed him to the ground. As he did so, he felt a strange ache on his back, like it had been him that hit the ground. *I really must be getting old*, he thought.

"First things first, kid. Then for you it gets worse." said Joseph between catching his breath. "Well, fast runner, eh? Let's see how good you are without your legs." Joseph fired two shots.

The kid cried out but then just looked around.

There was blood on Joseph's legs. He looked at the kid, then collapsed on the ground grabbing his gunshot legs. The kid was looking past him to someone behind him. Joseph had to know. He turned to see a homeless man watching. The man had his hands in his pockets. Did he fire the gun?

The driver ran over from the car, and the kid ran in the opposite direction, past the homeless guy, stopping for a quick word before continuing. Joseph was losing consciousness but something wasn't right. Was the homeless man an undercover cop?

"Take a photo of that homeless guy," said Joseph. The driver aimed his phone, but the camera wouldn't capture a picture. He tried a few times and then called back to his boss, "My phone's broken. Do you have yours?"

Joseph could see the homeless man leaving and could hear approaching sirens just before everything went black.

Emily's attack

Joseph wasn't in hospital long. He had nothing to say to the police and couldn't help them with their enquiries. His men had located the kid's house, but his parents had moved him out of the city. He wasn't happy that the kid, Ricky, had apparently gotten away, but he didn't have an issue with his family. The family were told they were lucky to get off with a warning.

Joseph was focused on who the homeless man/undercover policeman was. He must have been the shooter as the kid didn't have any weapons. Contracts were issued and it took a week to track the whereabouts of the homeless man. No one ever noticed homeless people. They discovered he liked to sleep near the fountain and the contract stipulated he was to be taken in alive. Joseph had a score to settle.

Peter was assigned to the contract. He was a career criminal and was ruthless. He wasn't happy to be bringing in a man alive, but he could do it if the man co-operated. He arrived at the fountain, late at night so there wouldn't be any witnesses. He looked for his target. A lady stepped out of a nearby restaurant and then he spotted his mark. "This lady just happens to be at the wrong place at the wrong time," he said under his breath.

He didn't want to kill her in case the homeless man truly was an undercover policeman, so he decided he would slash the lady and then take the homeless man with less resistance. Peter walked straight up to the lady as she came out of the restaurant and without saying a word, he lunged at her slashing his knife deep across her arm. But she didn't fall.

He noticed his own pain; first a heart attack and then he screamed in agony with the pain of the bleeding gash on his own arm. He fell to the ground clutching his arm in shock. The man told the lady to leave then just stood there with his hands in his pocket.

"What did you do? My boss warned me about you! Who are you?"

A restaurant worker looked through the window and reached for the phone.

Chapter Nine

Emily was seated at her desk when a now familiar feeling frisked through her heart. *What could he be doing here?* thought Emily. She looked up and was surprised to see John standing in the doorway of her office.

"Hi John. Where did you come from?"

"What? Why do you ask?" replied John.

"My office is hard to find and usually someone from reception will announce visitors and then bring them to me."

"Oh, you're asking about now," replied John, offering no further explanation.

"Come in and sit down. How can I help?"

Emily let the homeless people she spoke direct all contact as she didn't want to scare them. John sat down. As Ashley had explained, John's appearance was clean and he didn't look scruffy or unshaven. "Roger told me you had left."

"Yes, but not indefinitely. I've just temporarily relocated to another part of town."

"If you've spoken to Roger, are you hear to answer my questions?"

"No," replied John.

Emily was disappointed with the reply, but at least it wasn't cryptic. Emily assumed that John's motive was to use the services of the Foundation and waited to be guided on what assistance he required. Emily started to gather some brochures together.

"I'm not here to answer questions or use the services. I've come to seek answers for myself."

Since the attack, Emily's thoughts had been consumed by the details of that night. Multiple questions, no plausible answers, a mystery with little hope of being solved. Emily was confused by John's request. She knew that John knew the answers, but here he was, seemingly just as confused as Emily was and also wanting answers.

"That attack on you was different than any other I've witnessed, and I want to know why."

Emily was annoyed but she restrained herself from showing her frustration. She needed to proceed with caution if she was to get any answers from him. "Different in what sense? Do you mean that I wasn't attacked? Have you seen others get attacked?"

"Different because of your reaction. You were being attacked but you were able to witness what actually took place. The outcome was also milder," he said.

Emily was frustrated and continued to probe, her psychology skills coming in handy. "OK, so these attacks happen regularly enough for you to deem me different?"

"Yes. Just one of the illusions surrounding you," he replied.

"So, just to be clear, I was attacked. The attacker was injured and I was not. You were there and physically did nothing. But I'm the one who is different?" Emily's displeasure was increasing.

"Emily, I don't think our questions will help either of us. I came here to tell you I'll be leaving for a few weeks. We're both seeking answers but for different purposes. This is new for me too," said John.

Emily felt that John was being sincere. "The other night, was it you who attacked that man?"

"No," replied John. "The man intended to attack you, but he bore the consequence of his action."

The conversation had now circled back to the similar answers John provided when Emily first approached him at the fountain. "Roger told me that someone like you will come and go. What did Roger mean?"

John was surprised by her comment. "Roger is more perceptive than I thought. He's a good man, and I've advised him to seek the services of your Foundation."

"John, I work with the homeless daily. You're very different to me as apparently I am to you. Can you give me the answers I need?" replied Emily.

"Emily, were you born in New York?"

"I'm sorry ...?" blurted Emily, not expecting the change in questioning about her personal life.

"Sorry to alarm you, but knowing about you will help me find our answers."

"OK, you didn't alarm me. It was just unexpected. In answer to your question – no, I was born in Indiana."

"You have a mother and a father, who both work in the Foundation. Are they your natural parents?"

"I'm adopted." said Emily, becoming wary. "Your questions have not got very far in knowing the real me." *It would be insensitive to pass judgment on me based on my parents,* thought Emily

"Did you have a normal childhood?" asked John, ignoring Emily's changing attitude.

"I was very much loved by both my parents. They taught me the ethics and morals that allow me to see the greater good. My family is extremely wealthy and they use their money to assist the community. I'm sorry John but are you also a reporter, trying to write a story about my family?"

"You don't have anything out of the ordinary? No special powers?"

"I really have no idea how to answer these questions. You obviously think you know something about me and are trying to find out if I am who you think I am," replied Emily. "No more mystery. I'll tell you what I know." Emily had tired of John's cryptic questions. "I can feel the pureness of a person. I didn't feel scared when you were there and my arm wasn't slashed. I don't understand what happened, but I just wasn't scared. I was more surprised and sad that a fellow human would do that to another. By the way, your friend Roger – he's as cryptic as you."

"Last question. I can sense when you're around. Do you feel the same connection?"

Emily nodded and explained the flutter in her heart.

"I'll be leaving today but I'll return with answers. Can you to keep this conversation private until I return?"

There was a truth to John and Emily appreciated the cryptic honesty. She knew that her word was paramount and agreed to his demand, advising him she would only mention this meeting to her parents.

"Emily, I think we will have much to learn. So to help you in your search for the truth, continue with an open mind and an awareness of your difference."

Emily was confused. "What is my difference, and what do you mean an open mind?"

John stood. "Your male friend, the one who gave me the food, will help you with your lessons. Listen to your intuition. I'm sure you have skills that you don't even realize. Analyze and draw a conclusion when you're together," said John. "Don't take him at face value. When I return, I'll be interested in knowing if you can foresee the consequence."

"So, I'm supposed to be with Michael even if it turns out I don't like him just to see if I can foresee anything?"

"No. Don't do anything against your will. Give the man a chance to see where it can lead. Be true to yourself and follow your intuition."

With that, John walked through the doorway of Emily's office and out into the hall.

"Hi again," called Ashley.

"How are you feeling?" asked John.

"Good now, and thank you so much for helping me," replied Ashley.

"Good to hear. Nice to see you again."

Ashley walked into Emily's office. "I know you're under a confidentiality agreement, so just a general observation," said Ashley. "Isn't he the most handsome man you've ever seen?"

Chapter Ten

Monday morning shifts arrive all too soon, thought Michael. It had been a great night with Emily on Saturday and he now needed to lock in the golf date on Friday. He would see Ryan at work so didn't have to plan the talk. As with most shifts, today Michael was scheduled in Emergency.

Michael went over to the triage nurse to identify the most critical patient and priority care. An Emergency shift ranged from a patient presenting with a broken arm from falling off a trampoline to a knife or gunshot wound, a domestic abuse incident to car accident. Lately, his shift involved many car accidents, falls, head injuries or different knife injuries.

Most patients felt very confident with Michael's dedication and professionalism. All the nurses were very helpful and attentive to Michael's request for patient care. His friend Ryan was on a rotating roster to work throughout the different hospital departments for experience and exposure. Today, Ryan was working in Imaging. As lunchtime was well overdue, Michael started to think about his hunger and getting some food.

As usual, it had been a busy work morning. Michael messaged Ryan to see if he was free for lunch. It was difficult to organize lunch routines with each other as patient care always took priority. Neverthelss, about fifteen minutes later, the two doctors met in the hospital café.

"Good to see you," said Ryan. "What a busy morning. Have you arranged another date with Emily?"

"Funny you should mention that," said Michael, smirking.

Ryan raised an eyebrow. "I've asked Emily to play golf on Friday morning so I was hoping I could swap?"

"That'll be OK. Once you and Emily are an item, I get Ashley all to myself so swap with me anytime you need. We can play golf the following week. You're probably due to beat me so a break will be good."

"Pretty sure I win as many games as I lose," said Michael.

"Just remember, Emily is afraid of commitment so we're all hoping you're the one," said Ryan.

"Yes, me too. She has everything I'm seeking: looks, personality and career," said Michael.

"Good. Now that the romance is back on track I want to ask your advice on something else."

"Sounds serious. How can I help?"

"I was thinking of applying for the South African appointment. What do you think?"

"When do applications close, and when do they announce the successful candidate?" asked Michael.

"In about a week, and it's announced in one month's time. Then you have up to one month to move to South Africa."

"Does Ashley know?" asked Michael.

"No, I thought I'd wait for the announcement and if I'm successful we can discuss it then."

"I've always known that medicine and helping others is your dedication. If I know it, then after so long with Ashley and as a doctor herself, she knows it too. Go ahead and apply. I can only wish you success."

"Thanks Michael. I'll put my submission together this week. I think I need you to endorse it."

"No worries. I know Doctor Newell would if he could, but as CEO he has to remain impartial."

Lunch was half an hour and as doctors, they could never let their team down. They spent exactly twenty-five minutes in the café and then said their goodbyes.

Michael pulled out his cell phone as he walked back to his department. "Golf is all arranged. Will call you tonight," he texted Emily.

* * *

Emily received had a spare ten minutes, so returned Michael's text with a phone call.

"I just wanted to say thank you for organizing golf. I have a spare ten minutes if you do as well."

"I can do five then I'm due back at work," said Michael. "With my roster, I'm usually sending and replying to texts, so thank you for getting back to me with a call."

"To be honest, I wasn't sure you would answer and I would have left a message, but I'll text you from now on," replied Emily.

"It's great to hear your voice," said Michael and Emily in unison.

"I told Ash we had so much in common." laughed Emily.

"Apparently more than we knew," said Michael, laughing also. "Emily, should I make all the arrangements for our Friday golf? Did you want me to pick you up?"

"Thank you but I was planning to use the corporate car. I like to get as much work in as I can and Chadi needs to complete as many driver hours as he can to keep his job. So it's a win/win for both of us."

"Is that Doctor Newell's chauffer car?"

"Yes, it came as a benefit with Dad's CEO position. Dad originally said no but soon realized Chadi would lose his job, so we all work together to keep Chadi busy. He drives many of the Foundation clients around and they love it as much as Chadi. I get where I want to go and usually get so much work done in that back seat that it's turning into a fourth office."

"Emily if you have four offices, you do way too much work. What does your work involve?" asked Michael.

"I'm completing my residency for psychology. The Foundation work provides so much experience. I have a strange natural ability that I can identify a person's true intentions, so I definitely picked the right career."

"OK then. What are my true intentions?" asked Michael.

"I know that you're a good person and use your medical profession to help others. Maybe we'll talk about it on Friday. Remember I'm also trying to use your doctor hands in my work," hinted Emily.

"They are available for you, for anything," said Michael. "Emily, I hate to leave you, but I have to get ready for my shift. I'll text you when I can and will lock in the golf details on Thursday. Thank you again for the call."

"OK, thanks. I'll see you on Friday."

Chapter Eleven

Emily was up early on Friday morning so she could exercise for a warm up before the golf game. Emily knew from Ashley, via Ryan, that Michael was very competitive and would make Emily work hard for a win. When she was finished, Chadi rang Emily's cell to confirm that he would drive her to the golf club.

"Hi Emily, nice to see you," said Chadi as he started the ignition.

"Hi Chadi, always nice to see you. I have a great deal of work to do though," replied Emily to advise him that she wouldn't be able to engage in much conversation.

The traffic was better than anticipated and Chadi pulled into the golf course carpark with time to spare.

"Chadi, I have between twenty and thirty minutes before Michael arrives. Is it OK if I stay in the car working or do you have somewhere else you need to be?"

"No Emily," replied Chadi. "I can sit here for thirty minutes, then drive away and come back when planned."

"Thank you." Emily continued with her work. Emily was so used to working in the car and had updated four case files before Michael arrived.

"Chadi, I'll just leave my work on the back seat. We're planning nine holes, so we should be finished just after an hour, but then there is coffee. I should be ready around ten-thirty for you to come and get me. If there are any changes, I'll call you," said Emily. She waved at Michael. "Hello Michael." Emily carried her golf clubs over to him.

"I see you have no buggy."

"I really wanted to drive around the course so there was no need."

"Are you in a hurry to get away from me?"

"No, I just love driving the golf cart." Emily was eager to start the date. She wanted to take notice of John's advice and try to work out the meaning behind it. Emily drove to the first tee and their date started.

As they moved along to each hole, Emily was surprised that Michael wasn't as good at golf as she had expected, it became obvious that he was allowing her to win. She had expected him to be more confident. "Michael, there's no need to play badly. I'll beat you fair and square. But apologies if you really are that bad." Emily squealed with laughter.

"Sorry," said Michael, "I'll play properly and beat you fair and square."

They turned out to be evenly matched and the game became very competitive. They both enjoyed each other's company, laughed at Emily's speed/slow/stop driving and spoke constantly. They wanted to know as much as they could about each other.

"Emily, even though I'm winning this game, I'm interested in knowing more about the Foundation so I can work out where I can fit in," said Michael.

"Our game isn't over. You haven't won," Emily halfheartedly joked. "But seriously. My parents and I manage the Foundation and we all, including Ashley, work to help in any way we can. Ashley is preparing to open another branch."

"Can you tell me more about what your dad does there?" he asked.

Michael seemed to ask a lot of questions about her dad. She was happy to see the respect Michael had for him, but she had remembered her thoughts on their first date. And she also remembered the conversation she'd had with John. *Had John meant that Michael's motivates are wrong?* thought Emily. Emily had tried not to focus on John's cryptic conversation. Her logic told her it was irrational, but her instincts said otherwise. Emily started dissecting every question and answer rather than enjoying Michael's company.

"Dad takes his job at the hospital seriously. He is the Chief Executive Officer and he prioritizes his work duties. Dad set up educational scholarships for the Foundation and, where possible, he will try and help at the Foundation. Dad and you would work very well together. You both respect each other," said Emily.

"So, what does Emily Newell do?"

Emily was glad he'd picked up on her change of tone and changed the subject. "Well, it's about time we got to me!" joked Emily. "My residency is my priority now so I don't take on cases that I cannot finalize as it's not fair on our clients."

Michael said he was taken aback by the selflessness of the Newell family. He had never met people of their wealth who gave so much back to the community. Michael said he could offer his services to the Foundation when it fitted in with his schedule. Emily knew the promise, although sweet, was empty. Michael's conversations appeared calculated and Emily wasn't sure if they were to win Emily over or gain points with Martin.

As they continued their way around the course, there were plenty of questions, laughs and banter. Conversations came naturally and Emily was having fun. The more they played, the more Emily forgot about John. Emily could enjoy Michael without an interrogation. At the last hole, they pulled out their clubs and took their shots.

"Emily, this has been a terrific opportunity to get to know you. Shame I'm about to beat you," said Michael. He looked over at Emily and smiled. Michael took his last shot. He swung the club and watched the ball land neatly on the green, leaving Emily with a very difficult shot to beat.

Emily was sporty and hence competitive. Emily took a longer time with this last tee. She looked at Michael. "No pressure," she added, as she placed the ball on the tee and slowly studied it and the green. Emily swung the club hoping for the ball to land on the green as did Michael's. They both watched the ball land on the green, circle to the right and then curve ever so slowly into the hole. It was a hole in one.

She gave a big smile and did a little victory dance. "That, Michael, is what you do when you beat me. Short victory and then we move on."

"Personally, Emily, I wouldn't have done the victory dance but now the challenge is on. Next time I'll be doing the dance."

As they made their way to the green to retrieve the ball, Emily looked at her watch. She still had forty minutes until Chadi arrived and didn't want to call him earlier to finish the date. "Do you have time for coffee or do you have to head off?"

"I've no plans to leave and I'm not ready to go," said Michael.

Emily made her way back to the clubhouse to return the cart, while Michael took their clubs to the trunk of his car. When Michael returned, they walked back into the coffee shop, found a vacant table and sat down side by side.

"Thank you, Emily, for joining me today. Although I think I may have had a better chance of winning if I had played with Ryan! Maybe we should ask them next time."

"Ashley would be lucky to know how to hold a club let alone swing it."

The waitress took their order and they leant in and kissed each other. She returned with the two cups of coffee and placed them on the table. Emily and Michael sipped their coffee in between conversation, laughter and kisses.

"So as part of the 'get to know Emily' plan," laughed Michael, "what haven't I learnt from you today? Annoyances, favorites, unusual behaviors, pets?"

"I don't know if we have enough time to go through the checklist, but let's see if I can give you some details. Annoyances … bad manners, favorites … chocolate, unusual behaviors … apparently my victory dance is unusual," Emily laughed, "As for pets … well, that maybe goes hand in hand with unusual behaviors." Emily frowned. "I don't own a pet. I never have. Once I wanted a dog. My parents tried different rescues centers, but laugh, if you wish dogs seem to dislike me."

Michael said he had never heard of dogs having a phobia of humans.

"Michael, this is serious. When I was little, my parents took me to the dog home to buy a puppy. There was not one dog that would come near me. As a child, I was extremely upset."

Michael shrugged his shoulders and softened his approach, "Well, dogs may pull away from you but I won't." he said, pulling Emily in for another kiss.

Their time together ended quickly. Their coffees were finished and Chadi was on his way back. They walked to Michael's car to retrieve the golf clubs. Michael reached for Emily's hand. Instantly she felt the warmth of his masculine hands and John's warning words flooded back. The kisses they had shared were very sensual and desirable, but Emily was still thinking of her father. "Thank you, Michael, I've had another fun time with you."

"I also enjoy being with you. We get on so well. I'll text you tonight and let you know my schedule and see if you're free for another date," said Michael.

"I look forward to your text and our next date," said Emily.

Michael lifted Emily's golf clubs out of the boot of his car, put them on the ground and shut the boot. Michael picked up the clubs to hand them to Emily but they fell together and into another kiss, and the golf clubs fell to the ground.

Chadi drove up beside Michael's car, catching sight of Michael and Emily's kiss. He got out and walked around to the passenger side.

"Hi Emily. Sorry I'm a bit late," said Chadi loudly as he walked around the car.

"Hi Chadi, thank you. This is Michael. Michael, this is Chadi."

The men nodded. "Good to meet you," they said. Michael handed the clubs to Chadi.

"I must go now. Thank you for a really good game," said Emily, staring into Michael's eyes.

"Goodbye. Thank you and I'll be in touch very soon," said Michael, returning Emily's gaze. Chadi started the car, reversed and turned out of the carpark. Emily turned to look out of the rear window and waved to Michael for as long as he was in view.

* * *

That evening, Ashley was home so they discussed the details of Emily's date. Emily explained that the date was interesting. It had been ages since she was out with a man and Michael was the whole deal; possibly the best kisser Emily had ever been with. She had been impressed with his golf game, plus he was incredibly handsome and had an attractive sense of humor. Emily had not mentioned her meeting with John, or their strange discussion. "I hope Michael is genuine, but something tells me he isn't," said Emily.

Ashley sighed, "Here we go again, another man judged before he even has a chance. You don't have many friends Em, not because you're not likeable, but you're so cautious! You're going to be a lonely old woman in a big house."

"Ash, I'm not just going to get in a relationship with someone just because I fear being alone. It's not fair on the person or on me."

"No one can give you one reason to stay away from Michael. I'm not saying you have to be serious, just give him a chance," said Ashley. "You do know Michael is a catch."

"I know Ashley. You're lucky to have found a true gentleman like Ryan," replied Emily. Emily had admired Ryan's innocence. He was a humanitarian. In Emily's eyes, this was a satisfying accomplishment. Money is not an achievement, it's a luxury.

"He so is," said Ashley with a smile. Ashley and Ryan were a cute couple. They were perfect, sometimes too perfect. Ryan brought the best out of Ashley. As did Emily. Ashley, wasn't as confident as she appeared to be; her personality was easily swayed by people closest to her. Ryan was Ashley's first boy-friend. They had met at medical school, first becoming friends.

Emily's cell phone received a text, breaking her musing. "Would you like to go to the Gala Awards in three weeks' time?" It was from Michael.

"Am I being too judgmental?" Emily asked. She felt silly. Michael deserved a chance. Emily did think Michael had poten-tial and everyone spoke highly of him. Just for once she would go with the group consensus. Without saying a word to Ashley, Emily texted Michael, "Yes to Gala Awards. Thank you." Emily then showed Ashley Michael's message and her reply. She knew Ashley would appreciate the event more than Emily.

"Are you serious!" exclaimed Ashley.

"I knew you of all people would be glad about my next big date. More so than me," said Emily

Ashley shrugged. "I have no idea what you mean?"

Emily had attended many formal events in her life but none as prestigeous as an awards night. "It's the first time I've attended such a night and I'm excited at the thought. I may even see an actor or actress I recognize."

"So, I assume you have a spare ticket for me?"

"Sorry Ash. Watch it on TV and I'll wave to you."

"Why would Michael be invited to a Gala Award night?" asked Ashley, excitedly. "See, I told you he was perfect."

"Yes, I always wanted a man who could take me to a Gala Award night," said Emily sarcastically.

"What are you going to wear? I'll come with you."

"I'm not buying a new dress. The charity event dress will do. It was very expensive and I'm not on the red carpet or getting an award. I don't need to be the star of the parade."

"Em, have you seen what the stars wear at these events? You can't wear that dress. You will look out of place."

"I'm not prepared to only wear the dress once. I couldn't believe how expensive it was. I was really shocked when you told me. I've seen what the actresses wear, but Ash, I'm not an actress. I'll not be on the red carpet so who will notice me?"

Ashley loved reading the gossip magazines and would always tell Emily the latest social news, mixed with her fashion critique. Emily sat and listened to Ashley's detailed description of an awards night. Emily realized that she was more enthusiastic about the new event experience rather than spending time with Michael.

Chapter Twelve

Michael had invited Emily to the Gala event without the approval of his overbearing, pretentious mother Susan. He called his mother after Emily had accepted. "Mom, I would like to invite Emily to the Gala Awards. I know she can only go if you approve of her. I just need to work out the family dinner date so you can meet her."

"Have you already asked her?" asked Susan.

"No," Michael lied.

"You are welcome to come this Thursday or the following."

"OK, thank you. I'll let you know." He knew his mother wouldn't rearrange her social diary to see him.

"Don't waste my time Michael, I hope she's worthy," said Susan. "It will be a formal dinner so I can test her social etiquette. If you want to impose her on the family, you must make sure she's dressed and will fit in with us. We have a new Belgian chef and two maids have just been replaced so I want to test the new staff on a formal occasion before I invite important people over. I want to make the right impression on them from the start."

Michael thanked his mother with disgust, closing the phone regretting he could not tell her what he really wanted to say.

"Are you up to meeting my parents this Thursday for dinner?" messaged Michael to Emily, just half an hour after inviting her to the Gala Awards.

* * *

Emily had just finished hearing all the social news from Ashley when she received another text from Michael. "What?" she gasped. Emily showed the message to Ashley.

"Did you hint you wanted to meet his parents?" asked Ashley.

"No, they have never been mentioned before. Does this seem strange to you?"

"Michael probably just wants to get all the hard stuff out of the way."

"Did you warn him not to rush me?" asked Emily.

"He must really feel you have a connection. Are you going to say yes?"

"I'll have to, just to prove to you that I'm not judging Michael too early. It won't hurt me to start learning about the people in the social pages. They attend a lot of charity events, so we may have a lot in common," replied Emily with a small amount of belief in what she was saying.

"You will have Michael there so it will be fine. You'd better reply, Michael may read something into your long delay."

Emily checked her schedule and was free. She had secretly hoped she wasn't. Now there was no way of avoiding it. "Sure, Thursday is free," she texted back.

* * *

The night of the dinner came around faster than Emily had wished. Michael had constantly reminded her over the last few days that the event was formal. She struggled to understand how a dinner at his parents' house could be formal. Emily's instincts said "run" but she now wanted to go out of curiosity. It hadn't helped that Ashley had spent the week trying to convince Emily to buy a new dress. She knew from Ryan that Susan's expectations were extremely high as he had met Susan in passing and had felt belittled.

Michael had stressed Emily so much she decided to get dressed at her parents' home where she had her full wardrobe of clothes. Emily put on her dress from the Foundation fundraiser and immediately began to stress when she looked in the mirror. She called her mother as she needed someone to confirm her choice of dress.

"Emily, you look lovely and they will like you just like Michael does," said Patricia as the doorbell rang. Emily looked at Patricia desperately as they heard Martin greet Michael.

"Emily is just running a little bit behind." Emily heard Martin tell Michael. Patricia left the room and returned momentarily with a dress box with the lid still on.

"Ashley and I got this dress as a standby. I was hoping you wouldn't need it, but Michael is downstairs wearing a tuxedo."

Emily hugged her mother so tight and Patricia hugged her back. "Mom, I know you would have hated doing this. Thank you for always ensuring I'm happy,"

Patricia smiled, and said, "Always." They headed down the stairs to join Michael and Martin.

* * *

Emily finally appeared. Michael's eyes widened, welcoming her warmly. Time stood still; the walk to the car was a blur. "Emily, you look so beautiful in that dress!"

"Thank you. Is it formal enough?" Michael held Emily's hand as he drove, kissing it softly.

"Excuse me for one minute," said Emily. "I just need to text Ashley."

"Whatever you want," he replied.

"Love you xx," Emily texted to Ashley.

Ashley texted back, "My pleasure. Have a good night xx."

Emily and Michael never stopped talking to each other all the way there and the trip seemed very short. When they arrived, Michael remotely opened a driveway gate. The driveway led to a spectacular Victorian-inspired home perched high above the road. It was by far the most impressive house in the street. Its lawns were thick and green, not a blade out of place and framed by well-groomed green hedging.

"Let the fun begin," said Michael. Emily nervously laughed while Michael smiled, butterflies fluttering in his stomach. Michael drove through the open gates, up the driveway and over to the side of the garage. He parked the car in that location, hidden from the street. His mother didn't allow family members to park at the front of the house as it hindered the street view of the whole house, in its full grandeur.

Michael tried not to show how tense he was. Emily grabbed hold of Michael's hand and he relaxed a bit. I hope my mother can see Emily for her honest, inner beauty. He knew Susan wouldn't, but still he hoped. Michael smiled at Emily and pushed the doorbell.

The door was opened almost immediately by a uniformed maid.

"Hi, I'm Michael. We're here to see Mister and Missus Lister."

"Yes, they are expecting you. Please follow me," said the maid.

"I'm their son, I know where they are, so thanks anyway."

The maid followed Michael.

"Why did you not introduce me?" whispered Emily. "Why doesn't she know you? "

"Tell you later," whispered Michael back. He led Emily into the sitting room and over to his now standing parents, Susan and Oliver.

"Hi Mom and Dad," said Michael. "Emily, I would like to introduce you to Mrs Lister, my mother and Mr Lister, my father." He leaned in and gave his mother a light kiss on the cheek.

* * *

Emily didn't know whether to curtsey, hug or shake hands. Never had she been so out of her depth and yet so grateful to Ashley and Patricia for the dress she was wearing. She opted for a simple, "Hello Mister and Missus Lister."

"Hello Emily, good to meet you. Please call me Oliver. My wife would like you to call her Susan." Emily smiled at Oliver. She liked him and thought he would become a friend. He shook Michael's hand. "Hi Michael. Good you both could come."

Susan just stood there. "Emily, it's good to meet you. Would you like a drink before dinner?"

"Thank you. May I please have some water?" As soon as Emily spoke she realized it was the wrong thing to say. They had servants for that!

"I'll get it Emily, I want some too," said Michael going over to the inbuilt bar with a sink tap.

"Emily please come and sit here," said Susan, pointing to a seat near her. Emily sat down near Susan. Michael brought over a glass of water and handed it to Emily. He put a coaster on the table closest for her to place her drink when not in use.

"Emily," started Susan, "please tell us about your family. I don't know the Newell name other than at Michael's hospital."

"My father is the CEO at Michael's hospital, but both of my parents are very proud to be involved with their Foundation. They work closely with the community."

Michael and Oliver exchanged a glance. It made her uncomfortable.

"Emily, your family is well known in the finance sector. The huge family estate would make the Foundation a very strong and successful venture," said Oliver, more to Susan than Emily.

The maid came to the door and announced, "Dinner is served."

Dinner was very formal. There were four courses and each was very delicate and at the standard of a five-star restaurant.

Emily said "Thank you" twice, before she realized you don't thank the staff when they put down a plate in front of you or remove a finished course plate. Emily knew you couldn't have too many manners but it was making others uncomfortable, so fitting in was much easier.

Susan asked Michael, "How is your work? Are you still content with just being a doctor?"

Emily recoiled in shock at his mother's question and then swelled with pride at Michael's answer.

"Mom, you know I really have no interest in being a surgeon for the wealthy when I can be a doctor for the sick. I make good money and Dad is investing it, so I'm making really good money while living a very rewarding life."

"Emily, with so much family money, why are you even working?" asked Susan.

"There are so many people who need help and I really enjoy the work. My psychology degree is allowing me to help people. I would like to break the social circles and give people hope," said Emily, confidently and proud of who she was. *Surely she must realize how rude and condescending she is?* thought Emily, maintaining a neutral face.

"Well done. Your parents must be so proud," said Oliver.

"Has Michael told you about his very successful brother Samuel?" asked Susan.

Emily had her head down cutting the delicious meat on her plate. Susan had not used her name, but the question could only have been to her. "No, not in detail." She was surprised by such an unrelated, bizarre question.

"Samuel is younger than Michael but has achieved a lot for his age. He went to Harvard and graduated with honors in law. He is a partner in a law firm in Manhattan. His girlfriend is Alexis Green. You may know of her from all the movies she has starred in? They're a real power couple. Perhaps you've seen them together in the social pages?" Susan was beaming.

Emily watched Susan's lips move, but could not believe the words coming out of them. She hadn't met Samuel but would never compare the two brothers. She felt sick listening to how unthinking Susan was. Emily felt a profound sense of sadness for Michael. *This is why he was so intent on me dressing formal tonight,* thought Emily.

"No wonder you're so proud of your sons," she said as though speaking directly to Michael. A smile lingered on Michael's face.

The conversation continued about Susan's friends, the social economy and what an exciting daughter-in-law Alexis Green will make as she's invited to so many social events. Emily felt very grateful there were only four courses as the dinner was proving to be very long. Susan did most of the dinner conversation, while Oliver supported Michael with Emily. With the last plates removed from the table, Susan suggested that everyone move to the sitting room for coffee or brandy.

"Thank you for such a lovely meal, Mom. The new staff did a wonderful job," said Michael. "But, I'm working early tomorrow and need to drive Emily back home."

"I understand. Please excuse me Emily while I steal Michael for a quick word."

Michael and Susan got up from the table and walked out to the adjoining room.

Oliver looked at Emily and smiled. "Thank you for coming tonight. I hope you had a wonderful evening. Michael has spoken very fondly of you."

"It was lovely, thank you very much. I've had a lovely time."

* * *

"She can come to the Gala Awards," said Susan in the next room.

"Thank you, Mom," said Michael as he kissed her on the cheek. He loved his mom as did any other child, but the relationship was strained. Michael felt vulnerable when it came to his mom's own "truth." The family dinner had gone as best as could be expected. "I'll say our goodbyes."

Michael walked back into the dining room, and shook hands with Oliver. "Thanks Dad. See you soon." Michael turned to look at Emily. "Are you ready?"

"Yes, thank you. Oliver, it was good to meet you."

"Good to meet you also. Thank you for coming," said Oliver, staying seated at the table.

"Thank you, Susan, it was good to meet you. You have a beautiful home and a great chef."

"Thank you, Emily. I hope we will see more of you."

Michael took Emily's arm and they followed the maid to the door. Michael and Emily walked through the front door and back out into their own little world. Michael started the engine and steered the car in the direction of home. "Thank you, Emily. I know that was very difficult for you," said Michael.

"I know the answer to why you didn't introduce me to the maid, but why did she not know you?" asked Emily.

"My mother's staff don't last long. There's a huge turnover. The maid was new, so she had never met me," answered Michael. "Emily, anything you want to discuss about dinner?"

"Oh Michael, for the rest of the trip home, I'm sure we will be discussing this dinner," laughed Emily.

Chapter Thirteen

Over the next three weeks Emily and Michael fell into a pattern of seeing each other at least twice a week. It was usually one day date and one night date. This was the best they could do with their busy schedules. They played sports like racquetball, and went snorkeling and waterskiing.

During every date, Emily was laughing at her thoughts. On one hand, she loved the intensity of Michael's kisses and could easily have led him into the bedroom for what she knew would be a very sensual experience, but then she would get cross images of her father and her in a wedding dress. She still felt Michael had much to prove to his mother and that she would, in his eyes, make the perfect trophy wife which did not appeal to her at all.

As per John's words, she kept trying to hone her mental skills to work out Michael's personality and truth. Emily would fill Ashley in on the details of each date, letting Ashley know that Michael was worth the effort and she was really trying.

Emily and Ashley were spending the weekend before the Gala Awards at the Hamptons. It was rare for both of them to have a weekend free together, but they did it whenever they could. They had been doing it since college.

"What a beautiful sunny day," said Emily as they lay back on their sunchairs.

"I've been so busy lately. I've really missed the sun," replied Ashley. "Em, I've been thinking. I really think you should buy a new formal dress for the Gala Awards and see how it goes. We can both get wear out of it."

Emily was irritated by the suggestion. "Ash, I cannot keep buying expensive dresses, wear them once and never again. I know we'll both get wear out of them but, then again, if Michael and his family are more concerned about what I'm wearing rather than who I am, why would I bother? If I'd worn my fundraiser event dress to the family formal dinner, I'd be wearing the jade dress you bought me then. The dress you designed for me was beautiful and expensive. It may not be as flashy as what the actresses wear but it will be the most expensive. Plus, I'm not an actress."

"I watch these events and Ryan has told me about Michael's family. They are not the same as you. Expensive to them is important."

"You know me. Since when has anyone's opinion ever bothered me?"

* * *

"Emily, did I mention the award night is a formal affair?" Micheal asked one night on the phone.

"No, but yes, I'm aware that the event is formal."

"We'll be sitting with my parents, my brother Samuel and his girlfriend, Alexis, who is the up and coming movie star," said Michael. "Alexis is making the move from TV to the big screen and she is nominated for an award."

"I remember her. She was a TV personality. I read she'd made a movie. How exciting if she wins."

As the award night drew closer, Michael continued to remind Emily it was a formal affair. "Don't I look good when we go out?" Emily asked sharply on one occasion.

"You look beautiful and I'm sure you will look beautiful again," beamed Michael.

Michael enjoyed Emily's style; it matched her personality. However, Michael also knew his mother and brother's personalities and they didn't match Emily's dress style. Michael was confident that he had made the "formal messages" clear to Emily and now just hoped for the best.

Chapter Fourteen

Michael's family was very excited about the Gala event. They had spent the day preparing their "surprised face" reactions to Alexis winning the award tonight. Even Michael's father, Oliver, was cheering her along. Michael didn't have far to drive to pick up Emily as her apartment was within a few blocks from his. His brother and mother had called earlier to remind him of the importance of everyone's attire.

"Hello Michael. You do look very handsome in your tuxedo," said Ashley.

"Thank you. My family love these formal events," replied Michael, looking at his watch. He had told Emily that they all had to be seated before the cameras started broadcasting the Gala event.

Michael looked down the hall and Emily's movements caught his eye. He smiled at her beauty and then tried to freeze the smile on his face when he saw Emily was wearing the same dress she had worn at the Newell charity event. Without meaning to, he exchanged a nervous glance with Ashley. Ashley must know how he felt. *Please don't comment, Mother. Please don't be rude to Emily*, was all he could think. He forced himself back to the present. "Hello Emily. You're always so beautiful."

"Thank you."

"Are we ready to go then?" Michael hoped they could be parked at the Gala Award ceremony and seated at their table, before his mother had time to notice Emily's dress.

"We'll be early," said Emily.

"Have fun, I hope Alexis wins her category," said Ashley. "I'm watching the event on TV tonight so I'll look out for you."

As the door closed Emily said, "Michael, I really want to kiss you, but don't want to smudge my makeup. Can I take a rain check?"

"It will be a flood check. But I do understand." said Michael as he continued to rush out of the apartment and to the car.

"Are we late?" asked Emily.

"No, the carpark fills quickly. We have to be seated before the broadcast starts."

* * *

Emily had never seen Michael drive so fast. There was no real conversation and the silence was uncomfortable. *It's the dress*, thought Emily. *My feelings about Michael were correct.* Emily was disheartened. She had been looking forward to this event, not believing that her dress could be so important as to spoil the night. *Ashley warned me. Why didn't I listen?* thought Emily, wanting to jump out of the moving car and run home. She felt she had let Michael down, and Michael probably felt the same.

* * *

Michael was blind to Emily's beauty; his mother's inevitable rejection consumed his thoughts. He parked in the last parking spot. Crowds had gathered around barricades, cameras were flashing and the atmosphere was alive. Michael rushed Emily towards the venue, avoiding eye contact.

"I know we're in a hurry, but can we slow down a little before the heel breaks from my shoe?" said Emily.

"Sorry," said Michael, "I just don't want to be caught up in the crowd."

"Michael wait up," called Samuel from behind.

Michael gasped and stopped. He knew why Samuel had halted him and it wasn't a social hello. Samuel was with Alexis, his mother and father and Alexis' parents.

"Looks like you're meeting everyone now," Michael said to Emily. They waited for the group to catch up with them. Michael caught Susan's eye and pulled a "warning" face. Susan just smiled so Michael relaxed. He knew he wasn't off the hook; she would play coy for tonight.

Samuel introduced himself to Emily and then introduced the group members to her.

"Hello Emily. It's nice to see you again," said Oliver.

Alexis kissed Emily on the cheek. "Hi Emily, it's a pleasure to meet you."

"This is Alexis' big night," Samuel had used the introduction time to speak quietly to Michael. "Make sure you keep Emily out of all photo shots. Don't sit at your name card on the table. We had Emily next to Alexis, but Mom has taken one look at Emily's unsuitable dress and we don't want Miss Pauper detracting and creating her own news item. We're going in now, so don't walk too close to us. We don't want the media to know you're with us. Mom will change the table cards if Alexis and I get caught on the red carpet."

Samuel turned to Alexis and Emily, smiling. "Come on Alexis, we don't want to be late. See you in there Emily. Nice to meet you." He led Alexis towards the venue with both sets of parents following.

"See you in there, Emily," said Oliver, nervously.

"Yes, thank you, Oliver," said Emily.

Oliver shook Michael's hand. "See you in there, son."

* * *

"Thank you for joining us tonight," said Alexis to Emily.

"Good luck Alexis!" she said. Emily noticed the expensive and elaborate dress Alexis was wearing. It was gold, floor-length and figure-hugging. The numerous gold flakes were strategically placed for modesty and impact. It looked expensive and would stand out and be noticed on a very competitive red carpet. Of all the dresses there this evening, Emily's would have cost the most. It just didn't look it because it was understated. Emily felt Alexis and her could be friends and was starting to feel that in this family it was good to have allies. *Ashley would love Alexis,* thought Emily. *I'll try and organize a day out for them together.*

Emily could feel the tension between Michael and his family and knew Susan wasn't happy even though Alexis did seem genuinely caring and friendly. "Isn't Alexis beautiful in person?" said Emily to Michael, trying to minimize the stress that had appeared with Michael's family and not commenting on his mother's lack of communication. "Is Samuel OK?" she added.

"Yes, he saw how beautiful you are and warned me not to steal Alexis' limelight. So we have to just delay five minutes before we head in."

Emily liked that Michael wanted to save her feelings. Maybe Ashley was right and you never wear a dress twice with these people. Emily was determined to have a wonderful time at a great event with Michael. Michael looked a bit more relaxed. Oliver had done that for him.

After five minutes outside, Michael said, "You look stunning. Let's go in and enjoy the night."

They entered the venue, found their allocated table and made their way over to Alexis' table. There were only eight seats and Emily was very happy to be seated between Oliver and Michael. *Tonight will be amazing,* thought Emily. Susan and Samuel had not acknowledged her since meeting in the carpark.

Emily ignored the rudeness and was determined to make the most of this rare opportunity.

"Well, I consider myself to be a very lucky man," said Oliver as he sat down next to Emily. Oliver turned to a man seated nearby. "Rod, this is my son Michael and his girlfriend Emily."

Rod stood up and shook both Michael and Emily's hands. "Pleasure to meet you both."

Emily was taken aback by Oliver's "girlfriend" statement which made the relationship very real. Emily smiled at both Oliver and Rod, ready to enjoy the Gala Awards. Emily took in the atmosphere. She was honored that Alexis had invited her, because although the invite came from Michael, it was Alexis' night and Alexis' table.

* * *

"It's amazing, isn't it?" said Michael. "Thank you for accompanying me tonight." *Dress aside,* he thought.

* * *

"Let me know if you need anything," said Oliver.

"Thank you," replied Emily.

"Michael is really enjoying his work at the Foundation."

Emily hoped the shock didn't show. "We love having Michael. There is always so much to do." Michael was continually finding excuses *not* to volunteer. *Why did he tell Oliver he was working at the Foundation?* she thought. Once again, there was so much about Michael that she just didn't understand.

"I know you and your family are very wealthy and to be using the Foundation is a very wise money move. Your money will last longer and more people can be assisted," said Oliver, sincerely.

"Thank you. Some people just don't understand the good intention," said Emily.

As the night progressed, Emily found she could talk about any topic with Oliver and the conversation just flowed. There were many similarities between Michael and Oliver, although Michael wasn't as carefree as Oliver. Both had positives and negatives. Michael's negative was definitely his mother but Emily wasn't prepared to get between a mother and her son.

The nominations started on schedule with each category read out by a celebrity. After numerous awards, the presenter announced "Now, for the category of Best New Actor." A picture of each of the category nomination was displayed on the big screen. Everyone watched as the presenter opened the envelope. The whole table held their breath. There was a moment of silence – not long – but what would have felt like forever to Alexis and the other nominees.

"Alexis Green," the presenter announced, and everyone at the table applauded with genuine happiness. The camera was directed on Alexis as she walked from her chair to the stage to collect the award. The pride was clear on her parents' face. Susan and Samuel smiled with superiority, yet both were proud for different reasons. The award was an achievement for the Lister family. Alexis made a speech that was heartfelt and genuine.

"Next year that will be scripted beforehand by Samuel and Susan," said Oliver, quietly. Emily thought Oliver might have meant to think rather than say that comment.

When Alexis returned to the table everyone congratulated her. Emily could not but help notice the smugness in Samuel's voice. Samuel had not made a good impression on her tonight. He wasn't someone Emily would voluntarily associate with. "Congratulations Alexis! That was a lovely speech and a well-deserved award."

Alexis smiled with pleasure. "Thank you, Emily."

Oliver had given Emily his seat so she and Alexis could get to know one another. Samuel wasn't impressed, but again wanted to continue his role as the "supportive boyfriend" in front of her parents. The night ended all too soon and it was soon time to leave.

"Emily, I've really enjoyed you being here," said Oliver.

"Thank you, so have I," said Emily in return.

"Good, I was hoping you would say that. I know that Susan has a charity fundraiser planned in two weeks. I can't get out of it and I would greatly appreciate it if you and Michael would come."

Emily laughed and looked to Michael.

"I'll make sure I do a roster swap and we will be there for you, Dad," replied Michael.

"Thank you, both of you," said Oliver.

* * *

"I know I've already said it, but you do look beautiful," Michael said on the way back to the car. He stopped and kissed her. "Arh, I've been waiting to do that all night."

Michael and Emily talked the entire drive home, chatting mostly about the night's events and who'd won what award.

"So, what is your relationship like with your brother?" asked Emily. "I noticed neither of you said much to each other and that he didn't even say goodbye."

Michael looked at Emily and then back at the road. "It's complicated. We're very different. My brother is always conscious of his status in society. When Dad bought us push bikes when we were younger, Samuel refused to ride his as it wasn't the latest model. Mom fought with Dad for the same reason as Samuel. I loved the bike, but Mom forbid me from riding it in case the neighbors saw us. What I'm saying is Samuel and I are brothers but we're not friends. Our worlds are too far apart."

"I'm sorry to hear that," said Emily, feeling honored that he had been so open with her. They had arrived at her home.

"Thank you for a lovely evening." Emily stroked his hand. "Thank you for taking me."

"It was my pleasure." He leant in and kissed her. It wasn't as eager as before but still passionate. Emily got out of the car and watched Michael drive away.

Emily rushed inside, eager to relay all the details to Ashley. A note sat on the kitchen bench, "You left your cell phone at home. Staying at Ryan's." Emily looked at the time and knew her mother would still be awake so she rang Patricia.

"Hi Mom, I just got home and it was very exciting that Alexis won. Can you believe I was an embarrassment to them in my dress?" asked Emily.

"Did Michael say that?" asked Patricia, clearly shocked.

"No one said anything. They didn't have too. Michael was worried prior to his mother seeing me. His mother didn't talk to me the entire night and his brother didn't have to say anything for me to understand the message. I've been invited to a charity fundraiser by Michael's father and this time, I'll dress to impress. I hate being judged," said Emily.

They talked until Emily had calmed down and then they both said their goodnights.

Chapter Fifteen

Emily switched off the irritating buzz of her alarm. It was nine o'clock and she wasn't prepared to get out of bed yet. She burrowed herself under her blankets, wanting to go back to sleep but the details of the night before that had made her feel so inferior kept her awake. Emily began the slow process of waking up, stretching and yawning. The front door closing caused her to get out of bed a bit faster. It was Ashley and she was keen to tell her all about the awards night.

"Morning Em. Ryan was caught working late last night, so easier to meet him at his place. I didn't see you on TV last night."

"Morning Ash," replied Emily. They went to sit in the loungeroom. Ashley had coffees and toast for them both. "What would I do without you?" said Emily sipping on her coffee.

"So, how was last night?"

"Last night was certainly different. I'm sure Michael avoided every camera to make sure I wasn't on TV." Emily explained that the dress was an issue but didn't spend time discussing it with her friend. Most of the conversation was about who Emily saw, who she spoke with and what Alexis was like. While trying to remember names and faces through Ashley's prompts, Emily received a phone message, "Hi Emily, this is Alexis. Michael gave me your number. Are you free to meet me for coffee?"

Emily showed Ashley the text. Emily felt they'd had a wonderful time together and was excited to find out that Alexis felt the same way. She waited thirty minutes before replying, not wanting to appear overly keen. She genuinely liked Alexis and not just because she was an actress. Three days later, Emily and Alexis caught up for coffee with Ashley eventually joining them. Ashley felt starstruck and it took her quite a while before she could look past Alexis the actress to Alexis the friend.

* * *

A week after the awards night Emily and Michael were out on a dinner date.

"Emily, this is for you. I know you don't wear a lot of jewellry but this might go well with your new dress for the charity event," said Michael, handing Emily a small box. Michael wanted to make his mother happy and save Emily from any further embarrassment. Michael was giving her a necklace to make Emily happy and ensure that she bought a new dress.

"This is such a beautiful necklace. You have chosen one that will really suit me. I'll pick a dress to match it for the event. Thank you, Michael."

"I'm really glad you like it." Michael was very relieved that Emily was planning on buying a new dress. *Emily has everything going for her. Beauty, brains, personality, and if the outside packaging is so important why not dress up and just fit in?* Michael thought.

* * *

With the necklace in hand and an offer from Alexis to go shopping, Emily was prepared to buy a dress that would blow Susan away. After their successful coffee catch up, Alexis was now a welcome part of Ashley and Emily's friendship.

"Emily, I think you have begun to figure Susan out," said Alexis. "But take it from me, if you want to be part of the Lister family, you have to act like a Lister." Emily was happy to have Alexis' help. Alexis continued, "Now what I really mean is to act like Susan but not outplay her."

"Wow! That's intense," said Ashley.

Emily nervously smiled but she wanted to do this, although she was beginning to wonder if it was for Michael or for herself. She liked Michael, but knew there was more hidden than on show with him. She was really going through the motions trying to hone her skills as advised by John. Michael's kisses were so deep and intimate that her thoughts were still of her father and a career marriage so Emily knew becoming a member of the Lister family wouldn't happen soon. However, this new world and taking advice from Alexis was exciting and as long as Emily didn't hurt anyone, what was the harm?

"Thank you, Alexis. Where do I start?" asked Emily.

"Good," said Alexis. "As I'm sure you would have guessed by their rudeness, it's all about the dress. So, let's find the best dress ever for the charity event."

Now on a mission, the three girls visited numerous clothes stores with Emily trying on an endless number of dresses selected by Alexis and Ashley. Eventually, all girls were unanimous and settled on "the one." Shopping was demanding work and while it was never a passion of Emily's, she did enjoy the company and advice of her friends.

Hungry from their quest which they laughingly referred to as "Impress Susan," the three friends found a small café that was away from fans and paparazzi.

"Thank you, Alexis and Ashley," said Emily as she raised her glass and took a sip of her champagne.

Chapter Sixteen

The night before the charity event Emily dreamt of John. It was the first time she had thought of him recently. In her dream, they were alone in a glass box watching people walk past.

"Reflect on each encounter and draw a conclusion," said John.

Emily felt trapped. She tried to break out but couldn't.

"Let go of your reservations," John said.

Emily smashed her way out of the box slashing her arm in the process. She woke up with a start and turned on the light to look at her arm. She was surprised, thinking she had well and truly moved on from that night.

The rest of the day was spent with her parents, but she didn't tell them of her dream. It would open up the topic of the night she was attacked (well, if that's what it was). Emily had convinced herself that she had been confused and was actually a witness to the attack – it seemed more probable.

* * *

"You look beautiful," Michael managed to mumble after their passionate kiss at the front door step. He was speechless as he noticed her beautiful face, the dress, the necklace, her bag and her shoes.

Emily spun around slowly so Michael could view all sides. "Can't hear anything," said Emily to break the silence. She watched him smile as he walked inside the door. Michael walked into the sitting room and acknowledged Martin and Patricia. Once they said their hellos, they gestured for him to take a seat, but Michael was in a rush and wanted to leave. Emily went to the mirror to check her makeup and then into the kitchen to get her clutch.

"Have a lovely night," said Patricia. "Emily, you look so beautiful. Enjoy yourself."

"I will Mom," said Emily. She had been looking forward to this evening. Emily was keen to notice the differences in the types of fundraisers that Michael had mentioned when they first met. Emily never expected her partners to attend charity events, but this showed her that she and Michael shared the same values. She was surprised that they had never crossed paths at any of the other events she had attended with her parents.

Michael drove as fast as he did on the night of the Gala Awards, only this time he was smiling and the conversation was effortless. Emily was trying to predict the look on Susan's face when she saw her. She imagined Michael was probably doing the same.

"I've missed you," said Michael.

"Me too," said Emily. Neither had seen each other all week. "I spoke with Alexis today. We have become close. I really like her."

"Yes, Samuel told me the two of you had become friends and had also been shopping together. We're both happy," he said. "I've been looking forward to this all week."

"It should be an interesting night."

"Looking at you and how stunning you are in that new dress makes me want to stop the car and kiss you."

Emily laughed. "Behave yourself, Dr Lister."

"Ready?" said Michael as he parked outside the building.

"I sure am," said Emily. "Wow! They really chose a very fine place to hold the event." They walked towards the venue, holding hands.

"Yes, charity events are important. The guests expect nothing less."

Emily didn't have time to ask him what he meant, as they had reached a golden entrance. She assumed he meant that the guests were happy to spend more and give more towards the charity. Emily wasn't interested in focusing on the inner functions of a charity event; she was here for a good time and to help the charity.

The inside of the venue was more beautiful than the front. Everything was so elaborate that Emily didn't know if she was at a charity event or a wedding for someone famous. They maneuvered through the tables until they reached their allocated table number. Emily noticed Oliver first.

Susan was last to turn slowly with effort, her disgust quickly turning to pride. "Why hello, Emily. It's great that you were able to join us tonight."

Emily beamed knowing that Susan would now be nice to her and give her a chance.

"What a beautiful dress!" exclaimed Susan.

"Thank you. Did you notice the necklace Michael gave me?"

"Now I have. It's exquisite," said Susan. "Hi Michael."

"Hi Mom," replied Michael.

"Hello Samuel," said Emily, proudly.

"Hello Emily. We didn't get a chance to meet properly at the awards night but maybe tonight we will have a chance."

"That would be lovely," responded Emily. Emily walked over to Alexis and as she neared, Alexis stood up and kissed Emily on the cheek. It was obvious that Alexis was glad to see her friend. They exchanged smiles and compliments.

Emily was again seated next to Oliver and Michael. She was happy to have time to speak with Oliver again. Unfortunately for Alexis, she was seated next to Susan. Alexis was now an award-winning movie star and she was on display. Susan had obviously arranged the seating. Emily took Michael's arm and made her way over to Oliver.

Emily noticed Oliver's genuine smile and as she sat down, she felt compelled to kiss him on the cheek. "Oliver, so nice to see you again."

"Hello Emily. Hello Michael. Always good to see my two favorite people."

Emily took in the exquisite vision. Women were dressed in lavish clothes and the men handsome in their suits. Some people remained seated talking amongst their own party while others mingled.

"Different to a Newell charity event, isn't it?" said Oliver.

"Oh yes, this is so extravagant," replied Emily. She wasn't surprised everyone was dressed so expensively. As guided by Alexis, she had spent a small fortune on her own dress. Emily reflected that the amount spent on fashion alone would help many of the Foundation clients.

The food was four courses of five-star finery. The champagne flowed freely and there were auctions of memorabilia from vehicles, boats, holidays, sports, entertainment and fashion. Once again, Emily's side of the table conversed and laughed. Emily did feel sorry for Alexis stuck with Samuel and Susan. Once the chandeliers dimmed, people remained seated so Emily didn't have much of chance to move around or speak again with Alexis. The evening went by so quickly. It was continually fun and very entertaining. Michael had danced to different tunes numerous times with her.

At the end of the evening, the stage announcer came on to say $199,382 had been raised for the nominated charity. The crowd broke out with a rapturous applause and a representative from the charity came on stage to receive the check and say a few words of gratitude. Emily looked at the elaborately decorated venue and the well-dressed crowd. "Michael, how much were the tickets?"

"Don't worry. I've paid for them," answered Michael.

"Thank you, that's very generous. I was just wondering if they have made around two hundred thousand dollars profit how much the tickets were."

"Welcome to the world of fundraising," answered Oliver. "The tickets are two thousand dollars each and there would be two hundred people here. We have had world-class entertainment. The highest grossing female singer, Cassandra Blake, has sung her latest top three hits for us; the comedian, Dan Rochford, has his own TV show and he was well worth his fee; the chef was flown in from Switzerland so we all enjoyed international cuisine; and the twenty-six-piece orchestra that you and Michael enjoyed dancing to is actually based in Berlin. Emily, we always get the charity fundraiser crowd because we always get our money's worth at these events."

Emily looked down at her dress. She felt foolish that she'd worried about what Susan thought. It had made her lose sight of herself. Emily's smile left and she plunged deep in thought. *Let go of your reservations and learn your lessons.* Her desperation to be accepted had distracted her from listening to her intuition. She felt genuinely mad at herself.

As Michael and Emily left, Susan warmly said goodbye. "Well done Michael. I hope to see you and Emily again soon." Emily overheard Susan say to Michael.

Leaving the venue was a blur. Emily no longer took in the grandeur of the venue or the people. *How could I have been so naïve?* thought Emily as Michael drove out of the event and back towards Scarsdale. Emily was learning an important lesson. She measured Michael's reaction, he was impressed ... but not with how the event had turned out, he was impressed that Susan had accepted Emily. This whole time she'd thought that Michael wanted to be with her, he was actually hoping to demonstrate what a diverse person he was.

The drive was long and seemed neverending. Emily wanted to be home and out of "Susan's dress" and into "Emily's clothes". She didn't want to look at Michael, with his big smile never leaving his face. *Did he date me to get close to my dad or to tell Susan he was dating the CEO's daughter?* she now wondered. Emily tried to think differently, but it was becoming all too clear; getting his mother's approval was very important to Michael.

When Emily first met Susan, all she saw was the pride she had for the achievements of Michael's brother Samuel. Michael is now probably receiving some sort of recognition and would enjoy being noticed by his mother. Emily couldn't understand how she could get caught up in the social scene but tonight her eyes had been opened.

By the time Michael had driven Emily back to her parents' home and parked the car, Emily had her thoughts in order. When Michael parked the car, and turned off the motor, she tapped him on the arm and smiled. Emily tried to sound convincing. "Thank you for tonight," she said.

Michael turned to face Emily. He saw her smile and said, "Good, I missed you on the drive home."

Emily was now convinced she and Michael had no future together. Her instincts had told her that during their first kiss. With John's words now ringing in her ears, she realized her instincts had been correct. She had had a good night and didn't want Michael to leave upset. Emily leaned in for a kiss that she cut very short.

"Emily, thank you. I had a wonderful time this evening. Good night," said Michael.

"Thank you, Michael. It was nice to spend time with you. I had fun and you're a great dancer." Emily let herself out of the car and walked towards the house.

Chapter Seventeen

Once Emily was inside Michael sent a text message to his father asking, "When can I see you?" Michael wasn't prepared to give up on this relationship but he felt Emily was slipping away. He'd never worked so hard for any girl and thought a special intimate invitation could help to take this relationship forward.

Country clubs are known for their stateliness and only a certain class of people can be members. There was an unwritten code and acts of impropriety didn't occur amid the hard-drinking, wild-partying and cigar-smoking upper class. What was discussed in the Country Club was expected to stay in the Country Club. Michael didn't understand the culture and avoided the club as best he could. But today was different. He needed a favor from his father, without the interruption of his mother.

"Over here." Oliver waved to his son, standing up from his seat. Michael saw his dad in the far corner of the bar. He made his way to his father's table and greeted all the men seated with him. Oliver then excused himself and went to find a private table with Michael.

"I was waiting for the day you'd join me at the club," beamed Oliver.

"You know I like to spend time with you, but sorry Dad, I'm here to speak to you, without Mom around. I just wanted to ask for a loan of the boat. I want to plan a special night for Emily. Get on a Saturday and off on Sunday."

"Must be serious. This is the first time you have ever asked me to loan the boat."

"She may be the one," replied Michael.

"You have my permission but you know I can't say yes without first asking your mother. She plans so many social events around that boat and I don't know her schedule. Well for your plans anyway, I don't know the schedule. For my own uses, I always know the plans." As he called his wife he asked Michael, "Do you have a date in mind?"

"The sooner the better."

Oliver handed the phone over to Michael.

"What?" answered Susan, thinking it was Oliver.

"Mom, it's Michael."

"Oh, Michael. How are you?"

"I was wanting to borrow the boat." He didn't try to hide his tone from his dry answers. Oliver sat back sipping his Scotch.

"Michael, the boat is free in two weeks' time. I'll let the Captain know when. However, the Captain will be on board and our friends will be at the Hamptons that weekend. I appreciate it if you and Emily adhere to the proper dress code."

"Not to worry, Mom," said Michael, always accustomed to Susan's terms and conditions

"Good, then it's all yours. Text me the details so I can schedule in the Captain."

"Thank you, Mom. Bye."

"That was quick – congratulations?" asked Oliver.

"Yes, you know how it is. Luckily, Emily passed the dress code on two out of three occasions, plus I must ensure Emily maintains the dress code always or she could be an embarrassment and the Captain may spread gossip. Poor Mom will not be able to show her face in public, let alone the social pages!" said Michael.

"This must be getting serious," said Oliver, acknowledging his son's feelings.

"Dad, she's the hardest work with the biggest rewards. I want to take our relationship to the next level. Emily doesn't know anything about the boat. This will be a complete surprise to her. Thanks for your support. I'll have to contact her and see how this is going to work."

"OK, Michael. Good luck."

"Thanks for everything."

Oliver tapped Michael on the shoulder. It was the closest gesture to a hug that could be accepted by the Country Club men. Michael turned and walked out of the Country Club and Oliver returned to his friends. Michael was happy his dad had the Country Club and a good life without his mother, but really didn't want to end up like his dad.

He texted Emily on the way to his car, "Are you ready to enjoy an evening alone on our boat?" Michael started the ignition and drove home, convinced that Emily would feel special and commit to him.

* * *

Emily had spent the following day telling Martin and Patricia about the horrible charity event she had attended.

"That is why we don't attend those events," said Martin.

"We prefer to donate the money direct rather than exploit a charity using it as an excuse to socialize," added Patricia.

"Why didn't you tell me?" asked Emily, feeling upset.

"People are allowed to live their own lives and it's not up to us to judge their lives. This is a lesson you needed to learn for yourself. We are not to tell you how to live your life," said Patricia.

They had been watching TV when Emily received Michael's text. Emily read the text and then relayed the details to her parents. "Excuse me," said Emily as she went to her room. Emily had already called Ashley to tell her how horrible the charity event had been. Ashley always took great pride in helping to prepare the Foundation fundraiser and always celebrated in the profits raised. Michael's text had really surprised Emily so another call to Ashley was necessary.

Emily read the message to Ashley.

"Did you ask for an evening alone?" asked Ashley.

"No, I was really quiet. He may have picked up that I wasn't looking to continue this relationship and he's trying to save it." Emily was upset at the thought of breaking up with Michael. She liked him but she knew there would be no future. Their worlds were too far apart.

"What are you going to say?" asked Ashley.

"The truth and it will have to be now rather than later." The fact that Michael thought the way to win Emily was to take her on the family boat only proved that they were too different. If they went on the boat for a different purpose she would have found it romantic, but now it was a desperate move.

"Let me know how it goes. You'd better reply, Michael may already read something into your long delay," said Ashley.

Emily had genuinely enjoyed good times with Michael. She wasn't happy to end the relationship as it would most likely end their friendship. As John had advised her, she had constantly analyzed the relationship with an open mind. Emily now realized the interpretation of her dream. She was with Michael in his world and once she realized she was trying to fit in with the crowd that was watching her, she had to make the break to be free of the fake Emily and be true to herself. She must now wear the consequences of her actions.

Michael wanted too much, too quickly and for all the wrong reasons. Emily never liked having to break sad news to anyone. She felt the effect of the words from the recipient's end, but with Michael it was definitely a case of the sooner the better for everyone.

Emily texted Michael, "Are you home? Can we can talk?" A wave of guilt swept through her. Within minutes her cell phone rang.

"Hi Michael. Thank you for calling."

"Is everything OK?" he asked.

"I just wanted to talk to you about the boat offer."

"Yes …" said Michael with an obvious tone change. Emily could sense Michael's anxiety; it's what she'd been dreading. She knew the consequences of her words; the pain she was about to inflict.

"Michael, your life is very different to mine and I really cannot see us making this work. I'm really sorry. You want to strengthen our relationship and I want to end it. I'll have to say no to the boat invitation. Also it's time to end our dates. I would welcome a friendship but cannot offer anything more." There was more sympathy in her voice than she actually felt; a reaction to Michael's inner emotion that she was sensing.

"What happened? I thought we were getting along fine?" asked Michael.

"I know you realized I wasn't happy after last night with another formal affair. When I first met you, you told me how different our Foundation fundraiser was to the charity events you usually attend. Your charity event opened my eyes to a life I really don't want or fit into."

"The boat may be too soon. We can do other things and see how we go?"

"I don't want to prolong this. I can't hold you back from a life with a woman who could make you happy and enjoy what you enjoy," said Emily.

"Emily, I don't understand," said Michael. "But, it's your decision and I must respect that. Thank you for all the great times we have had over these past few weeks."

"Goodbye Michael and thank you for everything." Emily sighed. It wasn't as brutal as she had anticipated. She immediately called Ashley to relay the details, then walked back down the stairs to find her parents.

"I just wanted to let you know Michael and I have broken up in case you see him at work tomorrow."

"I hope you're OK?" asked Martin.

Emily thought she was, but she shook her head, "Michael was perfect – that is, the genuine Michael. But there is a side to him that I don't like. I'll miss the genuine Michael and I'm upset that I'll lose him as a friend," she said. "But he needs to find himself and be himself."

"Were there too many formals?" asked Patricia.

"That was an eye opener and I didn't like the whole business. The events didn't seem genuine, although I must admit I really do like Alexis and Michael's father, Oliver. In the end, we were only together for a brief time and there were too many differences."

"Is Michael OK?" asked Martin.

"He was shocked as I'm sure he had big plans for our future. I hope he can move on quickly. I know he will find it difficult telling his Mom!"

Chapter Eighteen

It was just past midnight when Michael eventually drank himself to sleep. He couldn't believe his relationship with Emily was over. Michael was normally the one breaking up a relationship. He didn't know if Emily could ever be won back. He was a doctor, had charm and could definitely get the ladies. He just had to work out his next move with Emily.

He really did like her. She was beautiful and great company. His dad liked her and even more importantly, Susan and Samuel were warming to her. Emily was dressing for his world and they really looked like a power couple. Her father could benefit his career, and with Emily by his side, he had a chance to outshine Samuel and Alexis.

Michael woke up in the morning with a very heavy hangover. He had to go to work that day as Martin would have thought his absence was due to the breakup and he didn't want to be unprofessional. He sat up in bed. There was plenty of time until his shift started, but he would need extra time to be early enough for a pre-work coffee.

I'll not tell my mother about the boat just yet. I have five days to try and change Emily's mind. I can only imagine the questions and accusations from Mom, thought Michael as he staggered into the kitchen, took some painkillers and then went through his before work morning routine. The shower may have been twice as long than usual, but he was able to drive to work.

Arriving at the hospital forty minutes before his shift was due to start, in a fit of an unplanned haste and panic, Michael decided to visit Dr. Newell, naively thinking that he may be able to convince Emily to change her mind.

"Hi Michael. Please have a seat. How can I help you?" said Dr Newell.

"Thank you," said Michael, sitting down facing Martin across the desk. "As you're probably aware, Emily and I have broken up. I would really like to try and get her back and hope my career mentoring from you will not be jeopardized."

"Michael, I hope you're not asking me to assist with any plans to win Emily back," Martin said firmly as a boss, rather than a friend. "I don't mentor doctors based on them dating my daughter. I was mentoring you because of your dedication and skill. If that continues, then so will my mentoring." said Dr. Newell.

Michael thought he detected a hint of anger. "I'm sorry. I really liked Emily and I'm in shock. Please disregard what I've just said. My work ethics will not change. Have a good day."

"Michael, Emily is staying with us this weekend to deal with the breakup. I suggest you take some time to deal with things too. I can see you're not coping with this well. You're an excellent doctor. I love my daughter and sometimes things don't work out. Our work life will continue as normal. Have a good day."

Michael left Dr Newell's office feeling happy that he had not ruined his working relationship. He admired Dr Newell's career and didn't want to jeopardize his own. However, now he felt more desperate than before as he visualized his mother's disappointment and vile words. Michael was frantic on the inside but professionally trained to maintain his physical composure at work. He wanted to go and see Emily to beg her to change her mind. Emily hadn't been clear on why they broke up and it was annoying him. As he had just found out, she needed time to get over the break-up, so there may be hope. *She never gave me a chance!* thought Michael.

On his way to the café for a much-needed coffee he noticed Ryan. "You're here early."

Ryan looked up from his seated position. "Hi Michael. Do you want to join me?"

"I gather Ashley has told you." He sat down at Ryan's table. Ryan nodded.

"Do you think I can win her back?" asked Michael, with desperation.

Ryan paused. "No, I don't." The honest words changed Michael's facial expression. "I'm sorry Michael, but Emily is strong willed and she knows what she wants. She feels bad for breaking up with you because she didn't want to lose your friendship. But that's all she wants."

The statement struck home. Michael now saw that it would be fruitless for him to try and win Emily back. But he could pay her back. His pride was hurt and it was blinding his judgment. "Thank you. I needed to hear that. So, what's happening with Africa?"

"I was accepted, I'll be attending a conference this weekend."

"Congratulations!" said Michael. "How did Ashley take the news?"

"I haven't told her yet. I thought I'll see how the conference goes and then tell her when I'm back." Ryan went into the details of the conference and the role expectations.

Michael didn't follow the conversation. Ryan had made it clear that Michael would never win Emily back and for now that's all that mattered to him. He finished his coffee and walked away. He felt alone. Ryan was unable to help him and Martin had made it clear it was over with Emily and didn't want to be involved. Michael needed someone's help and he thought of Ashley. He knew Ashley would be alone on the weekend as Ryan was at the conference and Emily was at her parents' home.

* * *

Ashley had been watching a movie and had fallen asleep. The intercom woke her. It wasn't late; Ashley had just worked that day. It was Michael. Ryan had told her that Michael wasn't coping with the break-up with Emily. Once he was seated on the lounge, Ashley asked if he wanted a drink.

"No thank you," said Michael. "I just need a friend. I feel like the outsider. You, Ryan and Emily were friends and I just needed someone to talk to. There is no one I can talk to who would understand."

"I'm so sorry that you feel that way. Emily herself would tell you that she would be happy to stay friends with you," reassured Ashley.

"I don't think that will happen," Michael said. "We all know that hardly ever works."

The silence was awkward. Ashley didn't know what to do and waited for Michael to talk through his pain.

"I can't help but feel that I was an outsider and that my family was too different to hers," said Michael.

Ashley listened as Michael opened his heart. "Emily did like you. She tried really hard to be with you and she gave everything to make it work."

"Thank you for sitting with me. I can't believe how lost I feel. I know we were not together long but I was planning a future together. Do you know if it was something I did? Emily never really told me why she wanted to break up with me."

"I just think, Michael, that she thought you two were similar in some respects but more different in other areas. I don't think you should be dwelling on this."

"I don't know if you know how it feels to be judged by your family," said Michael.

Ashley thought it was uncanny how Michael kept on saying things that related to her own experiences. Maybe they were more alike than she had previously thought.

"You see Ashley, it hurts. I feel Emily didn't want to get to know me. She just saw me as Susan's son."

"Michael, I'm here for you, but I think you're being unfair. Emily didn't do that. She doesn't dislike you, she just didn't see a long-term future with you."

Michael stood up. "You're right. Let's lighten the mood. How about I go get us those drinks?"

"I'll get them. What would you like?"

"Do you have any wine?" asked Michael.

She returned with two glasses and a bottle of white wine.

"Fine choice, let me." He poured the wine into two glasses and handed Ashley one. Michael started to tell her some funny stories from work. The conversation was easy. "You are funny, Ashley. It's nice having this chance to get to know you better."

* * *

Ashley was glad to see Michael start to unwind and return to his charming self. She was surprised to find that she quickly began to feel drunk. She had only had a glass or so of wine and was puzzled by the sudden effect.

"Wow! I must be really tired. I feel a little dizzy," said Ashley, trying to stand up. *Was Michael smiling?* she thought. She blinked and the smile wasn't there. Michael reached out to stop her from falling back.

"Here you are Ashley, drink this," he said.

She hadn't even seen him get the glass. She sipped the water slowly. "Thank you."

"I don't think I should leave you like this." He sat down next to her on the lounge and leant in, close. Ashley leant in and they kissed. The first kiss was exploratory, with each kiss intensifying in passion and need. Even in her drunken haze, Ashley remembered Emily's description of Michael's kisses. They were the most sensual kisses Ashley had ever experienced as well.

Michael wrapped his arms around Ashley and gave her a deep, sensual, passionate kiss. This would have been the most intense kiss; it was long, romantic and defining. While Ashley knew Michael was a very skilled and romantic kisser, this was the kiss that wound everything together for both. When they could pull themselves apart, Michael looked into Ashley's eyes, then picked her up and led her into the bedroom. Michael shut the door and laid Ashley down on the bed. There was no reason to shut the door, other than allow the room to fill with intimacy.

Ashley's hands ran from his back and up into his hair. She needed the touch to make it seem real. Emily always told her Michael's kisses would lead you into the bedroom and in this surreal dream, here she was in the bedroom with Michael.

Michael's skilled hands moved down her back and onto her bottom. He was the master and moved with precision and skill. Michael's mission was his partner's satisfaction and all moves moved in sequence to this outcome.

Ashley fell into his arms to enjoy the sensual kisses. They needed and wanted each other. The kisses became token so they could maintain physical contact while he stripped of his clothes and then hers. Their love making was tender, skilled and satisfying. Everything was intimate, slow, passionate and intense. They could not get enough of each other. It may have been the wine; it may be something else for both.

When they finished, Michael remained on top of her, cuddling her, breathing deeply beside her ear. He pushed up on his hands and looked down into her eyes, Ashley smiled and Michael lent in for one last soft kiss on the lips. He rolled off

Ashley and lay beside her on the bed. Both stared at the ceiling amazed at how perfect the other had been.

"That was exactly how I imagined it would be with you," said Ashley. "All the right moves in all the right places." Ashley instantly fell asleep.

* * *

The night quickly turned into the morning. The harsh sunlight brought the harsh reality. Michael had slept with Ryan's girl-friend; Ashley had slept with Ryan's best mate and Emily's ex.

Ashley lay in bed, staring at the ceiling, unable to look at Michael.

"Are you awake?" Michael asked as he turned to face her.

"What happened?" asked Ashley, not moving from her position. "I cannot believe we did this to Ryan." She had recently begun questioning her relationship with Ryan, and had always liked Michael – how he looked, the fact he was a doctor, his high standards – but *this*? She hadn't ever wanted this to happen. Not at all.

"I really didn't plan this, but Ashley, we both really wanted each other. You really are the one to decide where we go from here."

Ashley was surprised, trying to figure the events of the night. She was also surprised that she managed to get so drunk on so little. She turned to face him. "Michael, what we did last night wasn't something I intended to ever do. I've never desired to sleep with you. This was a horrible mistake."

"First Ashley, to help you with your decision, Ryan has been offered a posting in South Africa. He will be exposed to so many medical cases. For him, it's a career move. He's spending this weekend at a conference, preparing him for the move."

Ashley sat up. "To Africa? He never said anything about Africa." Ashley placed her head in her hands. "Argh, Michael what have we done? You're Ryan's best friend and you're Emily's ex. I've been with Ryan for three years and known you for two months. I don't know what to do. Ryan is leaving me. Why wouldn't he tell me himself?"

Michael moved over to Ashley and cradled her. "I won't leave you, Ashley. I'm still here." He kissed Ashley's shoulder.

Michael delicately placed his hand on her chin and slowly moved her head, placing his lips on hers. "I must say I always found you to be beautiful. You're smart, a dedicated doctor and a really nice person. I like you for you. You need to do the right thing by Ryan. I think you must realize that you and Ryan were over or you would never have slept with me."

Ashley sat in silence, gathering her thoughts. "I'll break up with Ryan and let him go to South Africa." Ashley was heartbroken. She had really loved Ryan, but he was leaving the country and leaving her behind. Emily was Ashley's best friend, her confidante, the closest thing to a sister. Ashley was overwhelmed with guilt. She knew Emily had never slept with Michael and she herself had never ever imagined herself with Michael … yet here she was. She felt she had betrayed Ryan and Emily.

"Ryan is back today," said Michael. "I'm due to meet him at nine for early game of racquetball. Did you want to come with me and we can tell Ryan together?"

Through her tears Ashley said, "I think it will be better if we speak to him separately. He deserves that I never meant to cause him any grief and I should be the one to apologize to him. Are you prepared for Ryan's reaction?"

"He's my friend and I owe him that. Plus, I do want us to be a couple."

"Thank you. I'm glad out of respect to Ryan, this is not a one-nighter. I'll also try to make this relationship work. We do get along well, we're both doctors, so we have the same ethics, and from what I can remember we're very compatible in bed," said Ashley, more to herself than Michael. "You're Ryan's best friend. I think he would appreciate hearing it from you. You can salvage a friendship with him, but I don't want to salvage a relationship with him. I can't believe he was going to leave me. I don't want to see him." Ashley was conflicted between being angry with Ryan and upset at his secrecy.

After Michael left, Ashley sat on her bed and cried realizing that she could not be angry with Ryan. She had been Ryan's girlfriend for three years and he was selfishly giving up his life to work in Africa. She had slept with Michael before knowing Ryan's plans. The breakup was her fault. She would try to be a great girlfriend to Michael out of respect to the three years she had just ended with Ryan.

Chapter Nineteen

Emily had arrived at the Foundation early today. She couldn't stand staying in the apartment anymore now Michael was with Ashley. Last night Michael had spent the night so Emily had decided not to hang about. Although Emily was over him, it seemed the genuine Michael was now gone. He was different with Ashley. Even though Emily had warned her that Michael's motives may not be genuine, Ashley seemed determined to continue the relationship.

Emily's heart flittered. *He's back,* she thought.

Patricia entered her office first. "Good morning Em. I have someone who said he has a meeting scheduled. A Mister John Lawyer?"

Emily looked behind her mother to see John as a well-dressed man carrying a briefcase. "That's right. Please send him in."

Patricia escorted John in and left. He looked at Emily and smiled. Emily stood up, leaned forward and shook John's hand over the desk. The feeling was electric.

"Please take a seat." Emily indicated the vacant seat opposite her. The room was silent. Emily didn't know where to begin. He said he would return and it had probably been two months.

Now she was staring at John the corporate man, not John the homeless man.

"I hope your mission was successful. Are you a homeless man or a business man?" Emily leaned back in her chair.

"I'm a homeless man when I want to be invisible. Now I'm a lawyer and will remain one so I can assist your Foundation." John handed Emily his business card.

She took the card and read his qualifications. "Your office is in an expensive neighborhood vastly different to the fountain. "You're such a mystery to me. I feel that I know you and yet I know nothing about you." John didn't seem as elusive as before. "So, will you answer my questions today?"

"Maybe, let's see how we go," he replied. "I have a mission and part of that detail is you."

"OK," said Emily, with curiosity in her voice. "So for now I'm to forget that you're a lawyer here for our Foundation?"

"Yes. Before I begin, I want you to know that I'm going to be honest with you, and I expect that for now we keep this conversation a secret between us. Telling people about me is against the rules, but an exception was made for you. I think you'll understand what I'm about to tell you. Whenever we are near, we can sense when the other is around. I've only ever had this connection with you, which is surprising. Actually, I'm from another dimension."

Emily was perplexed by the story unfolding and her expression froze. She was surprised that John was being so honest and although he just revealed something that would scare anyone else, Emily felt at ease as though she'd already known.

"I can see the outlines of human beings. White is a pure soul – your parents are white; yellow is your friend Ashley, and then there is blue and finally orange. Orange is at the opposite end of the pure spectrum. In some areas of the city, it can look like the night is on fire, blazing with all the orange outlines in the one place. I've been sent to balance the powers of evil. My mission is not to change the course of history, just to let different people feel the hurt for themselves. Whatever action a blue or orange outline tries to inflict on a white or yellow outline, they will feel the consequences themselves.

"I first noticed you at the car accident where I helped Ashley. What you don't know is that the car accident was caused by an orange outline trying to push an elderly lady into the path of an oncoming car. I've seen this before. When everyone is helping the victim, they go around taking bags and wallets in the confusion. They don't care that they have seriously hurt or killed anyone. The man who fell into the oncoming car was an orange outline.

"On that morning, I saw the orange outline following the lady and so I followed them both. I never know what's going to happen, but I need to be present to transfer the consequence so the good person doesn't get hurt."

Emily listened intently; it was a lot of information to take in. She didn't know if she actually followed it entirely. She remembered the car accident on the morning of the charity event and Chadi taking Ashley and herself home.

"Do people's outlines change? How do you get the correct color?" Surprisingly, she wasn't at all shocked to hear about outlines.

"Everyone is born with a white outline. If someone is moving from good to evil, the outline will change depending on their actions."

"Can people go from evil to good?"

"Only if they are not an orange outline."

"What if an orange outline attacks another orange outline?" asked Emily.

"I have no interest in the outcome so I don't try to help either."

By now, Emily had run out of questions.

"You are different. You have no outline. It really confused me. No one of my kind who has visited here has ever come across a person with no outline. I wasn't successful in my mission as I was distracted by you. After you came to me, I returned to my world and detailed my findings. No one can explain you not having an outline. Emily, you're now my next mission. I'm here to determine what world you belong to. You're not one of us, yet you're not one of them."

Emily sat still, trying to logically rationalize John's words.

"Did you listen to me when I left? Did you make note of your reactions with your boyfriend?" he asked.

"We've broken up," she replied.

"Were you able to notice him, see him outside of what he was saying and how he was acting?"

Emily laughed. "I don't even know what that means. You didn't give me many details when you left. I thought of your words often when I was with him. I saw a good side to Michael and a side of him that struggles. John, he's a nice man, but he's confused."

"Interesting. Your friend has a blue outline and when he was with you it turned yellow. The back and forth change of character showed his struggle," replied John. "I need to figure out who you are and if you have the same skills as us. You told me you could feel a person's goodness. I wanted to see if you were seeing anything physically change with him. Were there any lessons learnt by concentrating on your friend?"

Emily immediately thought of Ashley and was momentarily worried that Michael could hurt her. For all she knew, he was manipulating her and holding her infidelity against her.

"What about Ashley?" asked Emily.

John had not seen them together and so didn't know. "If I were you, I would watch them closely and try and help her without revealing anything. Please remember what was said here today is not common knowledge and your friend Ashley can never be told."

"I'm sure you could understand that I'm as human as possible," Emily said. "I do have an extrasensory ability to feel people and understand them on a different level, but that is because I'm intuitive and perceptive to people's behaviors and a trained psychologist. It's not anything extraterrestrial."

"That is why I asked you the birth questions. I've told the King about you and in his time of reign he has never heard of a person without an outline. He has asked me for more details. I've monitored you closely and my judgment is that you are pure."

"Thank you, John. I must say that my parents played a role in that," said Emily. "They have said that when they held me for the first time they knew we were meant to be together. It was like I knew they were able to help me."

"You talk about your adoptive parents?"

"They are my parents" said Emily, firmly. "There has never been any doubt of their relationship to me. I never met my birth parents." Emily was beginning to understand what John was trying to determine. She felt at ease with him and wanted to learn more and, in turn, help him with his mission. "I never got a chance to meet my birth parents or extended birth family. My birth mother died and my father was a doctor who was trying to save her. I managed to survive, but she didn't." Emily had not revealed these details to anyone else. "Unfortunately, her purse had been stolen and no one had reported her missing. Her identity is unknown. My parents tried, but all leads went cold. My father said her name was Lisa and that she was looking for a John, who would have stopped the evil, and that the man who attacked her was orange …" Emily paused, recognizing what she had just said. "John, enough! Tell me the truth. Am I connected to you? Was Lisa talking about you?"

"No, she wasn't talking about me in particular, but it sounds as though she was talking about someone from my world. I don't have any answers. That is something my leader is checking. There could have been a John on Earth at that time."

Emily reached for a tissue to wipe her eyes. "I'm sorry John, but I'm not just some mission. I'm a person and I deserve answers. Do you expect me to just accept this; that I don't who I know I am, that my life has been one lie after another?"

They sat in silence as Emily tried to absorb the information at hand. She didn't want to be rude; it wasn't John's fault. If anything, he was here to help her. She decided to change the subject in order to clear her mind. "You have said there is always someone here."

John cleared his throat. "There is usually one here at a time. It's not a good place to be a homeless person and we don't stay too long. I had completed my time, but failed my mission. Another one will be sent to continue that mission."

"Do you just come here?" Emily was trying to order the many questions forming in her mind.

"We go to different countries, cities and universes," answered John.

"Has some government power requested your leader to send you here?"

"No, we have very long existences and we try to help where we can. We're expected to improve ourselves and our near-perfect society."

"Does anyone in authority on Earth know you're here?"

"No, as a society you can be very aggressive to things you don't understand. That's why we come as homeless people. We're invisible and can assist. Surprisingly, the homeless are everywhere yet technically nowhere. In our own sphere, we're like a small shining twinkle. We have no form but we will automatically extinguish after five hundred Earth years. You could not stay here undiscovered, if you have that same life expectancy."

"How will you know if I'm the same as you? Will I continue to age?"

"We don't know. You may be one of a kind; more human than anything else if you have a human mother."

John had no answers. Emily was intrigued and continued on with her questions. "How do you get here from your home?"

"We just walk through a portal."

"You have a body and now a career. And use portals. I'm getting lost," said Emily.

"You need to see a human form and so I have one. It will be the same body, same age no matter how long I'm here. We always take the same identifiable form as the sphere we are in. Also, as I'm to stay here longer, it will have to be in a capacity to help you. So this time I'm a qualified, licensed practicing lawyer. The offer of pro bono work is genuine as it will suit both of our needs. I need to be respectable and so I have an apartment and place of work. We don't need to take the same time as humans to advance ourselves."

"Is your form a working body with the same human necessities?" asked Emily.

"Yes, I have normal body activities, but I need minimal sleep, food and water."

"With a normally-functioning body, could my birth mother have had sex with one of your kind?"

"I'll ask my leader and advise you of the answer."

"Why have you chosen such a handsome face if no one ever notices you?"

"We know we can, so we do. Usually our looks are based on many people's faces," said John.

"This has been a very enlightening, yet confusing conversation. After the attack, I went looking for you to find out answers. Never in my wildest imagination could I have come to this conclusion."

"Your parents have white outlines. I trust them with this information. They have loved you for your lifetime and they deserve to know we're watching you. I don't want to alarm anyone, but you're in an excellent position to assist and I can help you move forward. There is nothing to fear. Do you still feel safe with me?"

"I do feel safe. Was my arm not slashed because of you or me?" asked Emily.

"I'm not sure. We don't know if you have any powers. We need to investigate. I'll leave so you can talk to your parents. We'll need their help taking you forward. Thank you, Emily," said John.

"John, I'm so confused and I'm now feeling really alone."

"Emily, this was a shock to you, but you have much experience dealing with people who are lost and alone. Please talk with your parents first," said John. "Remember to help your friend Ashley. Michael has probably gone back to a blue outline. He's not orange but it doesn't take much." John stood up. "You have my contact details and I'll always be close by. See you soon."

Emily walked over to John and hugged him. Again she felt an electric charge between them. "Thank you. I'll organize for you to visit my parents' home. I'm sure they will want to meet you."

Once John had left, Emily looked around her office and felt out of place. All the familiarity was gone. Emily burst in tears, sobbing loudly. The shock that she was something different was too much to digest. *I don't want to be like John. I cannot live for five hundred years without my parents and Ashley,* thought Emily.

The news was scary. There were too many unexplained feelings. She stayed at her desk crying. Her world was changing and she may not be prepared. Usually she was the one in control offering assistance to people who were lost. This was a strange world.

She dried her eyes. She didn't know John yet somehow she felt as though she needed him. Emily needed all her strength and resources to help herself. She wanted the world to stop so she could get off, gather her thoughts and work out her options. Emily opened her desk drawer and pulled out a purse mirror. She wiped away all telltale signs of tears and picked up her desk phone. She buzzed Patricia's extension.

"Mom, are you free now? I really need to talk to you."

Patricia was already standing when Emily ran into the room. Emily hugged her mother as the tears flowed freely; she had remained strong for too long.

"Emily, what's happened?" her mother's voice was frightened.

Emily was barely able to get the words out. "Mom, the man who just saw me, he was the homeless man I told you about that I was expecting to return. He has made claims about me. He thinks I'm not like you or Dad." Emily pulled out of her mother's embrace and sat down on the visitor desk chair. Patricia wheeled her chair over next to Emily.

"Was he questioning you about your adoption?" asked Patricia.

"No Mom. He claims to be from another world and that I too possess some supernatural powers like him. He claims I'm not human, nor am I like him." Emily was almost breathless with her tears. "Mom, a few months ago I was attacked by a stranger. The attacker slashed my arm, but he fell to the ground with the savage wound. The homeless man John was watching. He claims to be able to see and stop evil." Emily knew it sounded strange but it felt good talking about it with her mom. "Mom, you know I'm not like other people. When it comes to judging a person's character, I've always been more … intuitive."

"Remember the story you told me about my birth mom, about John and the color orange? She was talking about the same John, except this John is in his late twenties." Emily could see this meant something to her mom and both women fell into an embrace and cried on each other's shoulder.

When they had finished crying, Patricia called Martin. "Emily has just had a visitor asking about her birth mother." They decided it was too important for a phone call and they would discuss this at home. Patricia and Emily gathered their belongings, said goodbye to the staff, and then turned and walked through the front door, waiting for Chadi to arrive. The sun was shining but the day now seemed very heavy.

"Dr Newell has called and requested I pick you both up, and then drive to the hospital and pick him up as well."

"That is fine Chadi, thank you," said Patricia. She turned to Emily and whispered, "We will not be discussing anything in the car. Please only say hello to your father and nothing else when he arrives."

Chapter Twenty

Conversation during the drive home was minimal as everyone was deep in thought. Once they'd arrived, Patricia went into the kitchen and Martin and Emily sat down together on the lounge. Emily started to explain the series of events over the past few months.

Martin listened carefully. He was worried about Emily. He had anticipated this moment and now found himself lost. He thought he'd be prepared but he discovered he wasn't. *Why now? Are they taking her away?* he thought.

Patricia gave everyone their hot drinks and sat down next to Emily.

"What I'm about to tell you will explain your birth parents and how your mother and I fit into your life. Before anything is said, I want you to know that we love you as our own and we know you love us as much as we love you. Our feelings will never change." Martin was fighting back tears.

"Emily, your mother and I decided that we would tell you as much as we understood so that when the time came, you would be able to have at least a few details. This is why you know of John, Lisa and the "orange." I'll fill in the rest as we know it.

"Your mother and I were working in Indiana; very content with our careers and without the distraction of children. I was a surgeon and your mother was a social worker. We had always looked after others and we wanted to concentrate on the less fortunate. On this particular evening, we were out walking enjoying the beautiful weather when we came across a young woman who had been attacked. We were alerted by her groans and screams.

"She was lying in a laneway in the early stages of labor with you. She was seriously injured and was rambling about a John and how he would have protected her against the evil and the color orange. As a doctor, I knew she was seriously injured, but first things first. I assisted with your birth while your mother called an ambulance. Your father arrived just as you were born and your mother died before I could help her.

"Your birth mother has always been our hero. She made sure she stayed alive long enough for you to be born. We have always loved and admired her spirit. You have the same commitment and many times over the years we have commented on your similarity to your birth mother.

"Your father told us your mother's name was Lisa and his was John. He was crying but kept saying he could not understand the emotions he was feeling. He said he still had a lot to learn about his body and that he was from another universe. He also said you were not due to be born yet and the attack must have caused an early birth as he would never have missed your birth. He said he could not take you with him as he wasn't sure you would survive, plus he didn't know how to care for a human baby. We thought he was in shock as a result of the grief, so we just supported him in whatever he said.

"Once Lisa was in the ambulance, your mother and I took all the details from the ambulance drivers. We would be completing all paperwork for Lisa's death and burial. The ambulance drivers were not keen to leave a newborn with a homeless man so we had to go guarantor for him and you. We had to fill in a lot of paperwork for about twelve months after your birth in order to adopt you.

"While I was completing the paperwork, John was asking Patricia questions. She told him I was a surgeon and where I worked. The ambulance drivers gave us some nappies and a small blanket to tide us over. We took Lisa's cardigan as an extra shawl for you, plus we really wanted a future memento for you. We still have it in tissue paper and a box in our cupboard.

"When the ambulance left, John handed you to us and told us he would find us the following day at the hospital and until that time he wanted us to protect you. We confirmed he knew what hospital and locked in a time. We then took you home, still wrapped in your mother's cardigan. We bought lots of times from the baby shop that night for you, but thought we would give it all to John when he came to the hospital the next day.

"As you can imagine having already spent one night with you, our newborn daughter, and handing you over the next day, was going to be hard. We had watched you be born. You'd only known Patricia's motherly arms. We could not believe that we had a child. The next day John came to the hospital as planned and I said I'd call Patricia to bring the baby down. John said that you were half Purifier. He said he could see that Patricia and I were white outlines and hence pure enough to care for you.

"We had no idea what he meant by Purifier or white outline. John suggested he could organize all of the legal adoption papers. Which he did. He said he didn't want you to be subjected to the life of a Purifier and so we formally adopted you. We didn't look for Lisa's family as we didn't want to lose you. Your father asked us to care for you and we wanted to respect that wish. We assumed your mother was from Atlanta, so we moved to New York and set up the Foundation which has grown beyond all our expectations.

"We wanted to keep you connected to your past and your birth parents and that seemed to involve helping the homeless people. The Newell estate was gated, private and isolated. We didn't know what the skills of a Purifier were or if you possessed any of them, so the estate allowed you to be free to explore if needed without the watchful eye of a prying society. As time went by and we didn't witness any out of the ordinary abilities, we were satisfied that you had inherited more from your mother than your father.

"You pretty much know the rest. You've lived a normal human life. You're very advanced in your learning and we have had to hide your IQ to avoid any unwanted detection. Physically you have the human capabilities of your mother so your blood tests have all been normal. I've always been in position to be able to monitor your health."

* * *

Emily cleared her throat, only just realising that, unknowingly, she'd been holding her breath. She exhaled and rubbed her hands through her hair. "I know there wouldn't have been a right time to tell me this and I'm glad it's all worked itself out to this point in time. I won't lie, it all feels surreal. I'm too emotionally drained to process the full extent of this. Only an hour or so ago my world made sense. The John that was in my office today implied that I have powers to be developed. He said he had advanced learning."

"We're sorry you received the news today, but we always knew our love would get you through," said Patricia, hugging Emily. "We had wanted to tell you on many occasions but we never knew who or what your birth father was, or what his abilities were. He was very cryptic and there were so many blanks in the story."

"This John is also very cryptic," said Emily. "I've been struggling trying to find out who he was. I never thought I was going to find out more about myself."

"What else did you learn today that I did not cover?" asked Martin.

"Nothing much other than the fact that the King was trying to identify John, my father," replied Emily. "This new John is staying to protect me and will be a lawyer for the Foundation. Would you like to meet him?"

"Of course we would. We have many questions. If he is protecting you and working for the Foundation, he'll be a big part of our lives," said Patricia.

"I'll call him now," said Emily as Patricia went to refresh their drinks. John picked up on the first ring. "You're here now? Do you want me to open the gate?"

Emily listened to John's reply then opened the front door. "You can tell me how you got here so fast later on." Emily led John into into the sitting room where her parents were sitting silently. "Mom, Dad, this is John."

"You arrived awfully quickly," said Martin.

"Yes, I used a portal," replied John.

"Well, John, you're always welcomed at our house no matter what your mode of transport," said Martin.

"Can I get you a drink?" asked Patricia.

"No thank you."

"He's not like Emily's father," Martin said to Patricia. "His emotions are not as developed ..."

Emily looked confused.

"Please sit down and we can work out what is happening," said Martin.

"Do I need to repeat what I told you this morning?" John asked.

"No, they knew I would get a visitor sometime in my life. My parents were there when my birth mother died."

"My father, the King, is trying to identify who that John is."

"Emily, you have a prince looking after you," joked Martin.

"Yes," replied John. "My father said she must be protected. She's special. She has no outline."

"We know she's special too," said Patricia, smiling, ignoring the remainder of John's words. "Maybe this is why you could never have a pet dog, Emily."

"Dogs can sense us and avoid us at all times," said John.

"Yes, poor little Emily found that out when she was two years old," said Patricia.

"We always knew you were different, Emily. When you went horse riding with Ashley and you both fell off at the same jump, it was only ever Ashley who was hurt. You have also never had a broken bone, but you always complained of pain in the same spot as Ashley when she was hurt. We assumed you and Ashley were just very close. Is this something to do with her heritage?" asked Martin.

"Yes,' said John. "There is a possibility that Emily was trying to save Ashley from the pain."

"Dad. I told Mom about this earlier. A couple of months ago I was attacked. A man tried to slash my arm. He ended up slashing his own arm and we're not sure if it's because of me or John."

"You were attacked?" gasped Martin. "Why didn't you tell us?"

"I wasn't hurt, but he fell to the ground with the slashed arm. Blood was everywhere. John was watching. How his gift works is if he sees the action he can transfer the consequence. But this time we don't know if he saved me or I saved myself."

"Interesting times ahead," Martin said looking at Patricia with a worried facial expression.

"I'm getting hungry. Is everyone ready for lunch?" asked Patricia.

"Yes please," said Emily and Martin.

"I don't need to eat much, so I'll join you for the company but no food please," said John.

Patricia asked Emily to help her in the kitchen.

"Dad is taking this hard, isn't he?" said Emily.

Patricia nodded. "Emily, the way your dad looked at you when he held you for the first time, he never wanted to let you go. You smiled at him as soon as he held you. He's scared Emily. We both are."

Emily gave her dad his sandwich and cuddled him. "I made your favorite."

Martin took a bite of his sandwich, chewed fast and asked, "John, what does your mission now entail?"

"Emily is my main priority. I need to help her develop her powers, whatever they may be. It will be in the best interests of Emily to work on developing these skills."

"I'll be staying here with my family. I won't be asked to leave home, will I?" Emily asked more for her parents' sake than for herself.

"No," replied John. "I'm not here to disrupt your life. We now know about you and we want to make sure we understand what you are capable of and help you to understand also. The King was very clear on that issue. Your parents are your parents. We have no intention of changing that."

Patricia and Martin breathed an audible sigh of relief. Emily was relieved that her parents wouldn't be hurt during this mission and that she would be with them forever. But forever is what troubled her. How long was forever? If she was like John she could outlive her loved ones by four hundred years. An average person would expect to live to their early eighties; some making it to their nineties. Whereas Emily now faced the possibility that she could live until she was five hundred. "And my longevity?" asked Emily.

"We don't have an answer for that right now. We will be able to work out your longevity as you age." John said, clearly lacking human empathy. Patricia reached for Emily's hand and held it. "I'll assist at the Foundation as a lawyer from now on. I still want to spend at least one full day on the streets. I don't need a lot of sleep and can use the nights to walk the streets."

"Sorry John, what do you mean by walk the streets?" asked Patricia.

"My original mission is to transfer consequence. Everyone has an outline. Has Emily explained this?" Martin and Patricia shook their heads. "White is pure and orange is evil. Yellow and blue are in between. If I see a bad person attack a good person, I just have to be there and the evil person will feel their action. I need to be present to transfer the consequence, so I spend a lot of time on the streets. I notice evil outlines following good outlines and stay close by for the attack."

"Is all this why we have been so busy at the hospital?" asked Martin.

"As the King's son, I did want to achieve greater results than previous Purifiers, so you may have been impacted with my casualty count. A lot of ambulances were called during my mission."

"John, when you were talking before, what did you mean by longevity for Emily?" asked Patricia, with a mother's concern.

John looked at Emily. "You didn't explain it?"

"No, it's too sad to think about, let alone say it out loud," answered Emily.

"In our own sphere, we're like a small shining twinkle. We have no form and we automatically extinguish after five hundred Earth years. Emily could not stay here undiscovered if she has that same life expectancy."

"When will you know?" asked Patricia with tears welling up in her eyes.

"Only as time goes on," replied John. "Both of you will have the normal life expectancy and then I'll look after Emily if she lives longer."

Martin cleared his throat, still holding Patricia's hand. "How will you help Emily develop her powers?"

"Emily will spend time with me on the streets. She will be safe and protected at all times."

They had been talking for hours and there were still so many questions not even thought of as yet. Everyone was emotionally exhausted, except John who was strangely emotionally detached. Emily looked at her parents and could see they needed time to themselves to talk about their concerns without involving her.

"John, can I walk with you now and leave Mom and Dad to digest the day?"

"Walking around this safe neighborhood would be a waste of time. If you drive us into the city you will get a greater exposure," replied John.

"What about your portal?" asked Patricia.

"I can create portals to travel big distances, but taking Emily through with my limited knowledge of her strength would be a risk I'm not prepared to take," replied John.

"Thank you," said Martin.

"The car it is then," said Emily. "Mom, Dad, are you OK for me to leave, or do you need me here?"

"No Em, you go and do what you need to do. Dad and I'll be OK. We'll see you later," said Patricia.

"OK. I'll park in the city, walk a bit with John and see you tonight. Is there anything you would like to discuss before we leave?" asked Emily.

"I'm sure we will have a lot more questions for John next time we meet," said Martin.

"Thank you for coming, John. While we've always been expecting you, we really didn't know how it would affect us," said Patricia. Martin and Patricia followed Emily and John outside. "You're now a part of our lives and always welcome here." Patricia hugged John, then Emily.

"Bye, Emily. Enjoy your night," said Martin, also with a hug.

John and Emily got into Emily's car and put on their seat belts. Emily hesitated as she was still unsure if she needed a seat belt, but for the time being, she would go along with the habit.

Emily drove down the driveway, happy to have John with her. "John, I want to thank you so much for being here for me. This is really weird and very scary, but knowing I'll always have you doesn't make the future seem as bad."

"Emily, you're my mission and I'm sure I'll learn a lot about the good through you, so we will both benefit," replied John, "The King made one thing clear: he doesn't want you to lose the human side of your life. He wants you to experience both ways of life and gain skills that no other Purifier has."

Chapter Twenty-one

As the sun set across the city and the workers were returning to their homes, Roger returned to the fountain. It was his favorite place. His life didn't have much to offer and he really appreciated the trivial pleasures. He was now regularly joined by another homeless man. Roger hadn't invited him, but with John gone so long he had grown tired of trying to keep a spot for him. The other guy kept to himself and didn't steal any of Roger's items or food and, as far as it goes, was an acceptable "roommate." The light rain had stopped and the two men were pulling out their bedding for the night. The bedding wasn't much but at least it was dry and warm.

The night felt still and silent. Wet footsteps could be heard making their way around the fountain, then stopping beside Roger. A man knelt down and whispered into Roger's ear. "My arm was slashed by your friend. It's payback time. You first, your friend and then the girl."

The voice was chilling. Terror consumed Roger forcing him to open his eyes. It was the man who slashed his arm when he tried to attack that friend of John's. Roger had seen the ambulance take him away and he had never thought about him again.

"Why do you need to pay me back?" asked Roger, staring at him in horror.

"Your friend shot my boss in the legs and then slashed me. You saw me on the ground and now it's your turn to be in pain."

Roger began to shake. He knew enough about John to know there was truth to the man's story. "My friend isn't here. I haven't seen him for a while."

"Don't play with me. I can see him right there," answered the slasher.

"No, he is different." It was the last thing Roger said and remembered before losing consciousness.

* * *

When Roger opened his eyes, he was surprised he was still alive. He saw the bright flash of a camera. His head was pounding and his hands were covered in blood A paramedic was working on him. Roger looked around; there were ambulances, police cars, crime scene photographers and the fountain was now taped off.

One of the policeman approached Roger. "Hi, I'm Detective Major. How are you feeling?"

Roger was disorientated and unable to think clearly. "Roger Lampoon."

"Roger," said the policeman, "you have an extensive head injury and will soon be taken to the hospital. While they prepare the ambulance, do you mind if I ask you some quick questions?"

Roger didn't respond. His head was throbbing and the policeman's words were a distant blur.

"Do you understand?" he repeated.

"I'm sorry, sir, we need to get this patient to the hospital," the paramedic said as he and his coworker lifted Roger onto the stretcher and into the ambulance.

"I'll need someone to accompany him. Sampson!" yelled Detective Major. The second policeman ran over. "Please go with this man and stay with him until I arrive." Detective Major spoke to Roger briefly in the ambulance. "Roger, is there anyone you want to contact?"

"Yes," said Roger. "Emily from the Homeless Foundation. She will help."

The ambulance sped away, with the sirens fading into the distance.

* * *

Not knowing where to begin their first walk together, Emily suggested they return to the fountain when it all began. An ambulance sped past with sirens wailing. Emily found parking a few blocks away. Both knew anything could happen between there and the fountain as it was New York. They walked towards the fountain. The first thing they noticed was the crime scene tape around the fountain. A policeman was standing next to Roger's usual sleeping location and a photographer was taking photos. Emily's cell phone rang and she answered the incoming call.

"Hello Emily, this is Detective Major. I have a suspect that has been transported to the local hospital. He has requested I speak with you. He is a homeless man named Roger Lampoon."

"I'm at the fountain now, where Roger usually sleeps."

"Me too. Is that you over there?" The detective closed the phone and walked over to Emily, bending to exit under the crime scene tape. They greeted each other, then as the detective asked to speak with Emily alone. They walked away from John.

"I know Roger. Why is he a suspect?" asked Emily.

"We have him on suspicion of murder," replied the detective.

"Murder?" exclaimed Emily. "Why is he going to hospital?"

"We're not sure what happened, but he has a major head trauma."

"I can't imagine Roger killing anyone. He's a client of mine."

"My friend is a pro bono lawyer for the Foundation. May we please direct all conversation to him?" The detective looked frustrated as the involvement of lawyer in any investigation was an unwelcome distraction. Emily sensed the detective's discomfort.

"He will not impede in your investigation, but he's particularly skilled in handling offences by homeless people."

The detective nodded consent, so Emily walked over to John and briefed him on the case. Emily and John walked back to Detective Major.

"This is the Foundation's attorney, John Lawyer."

John extended his hand and the detective shook it. "This is timely to have you here," said Detective Major.

"Yes, it would have been more helpful to have arrived earlier and been able to stop this unforeseen tragic event," replied John, diplomatically. "May I ask what hospital you have sent my client to?"

"The County Hospital. I'm willing to drive you there now if you like. I have a few questions I want to ask Roger."

"The Foundation will be paying his medical bills," said Emily. "We can take him to a better hospital. Can you please ask them to transfer him to the Royal County Hospital in Washington Heights, Manhattan?"

The detective went to the car and radioed it in. "The ambulance is heading to the hospital now. I need you to complete some paperwork, if that's OK?"

"I'll contact the hospital and ask them to send the paperwork to the Foundation. They know us well and we will accept responsibility for Roger," said Emily. "Detective, I'll also be adding John Lawyer's name to Roger's visitor list." Emily and John reached for their business cards. "These are our cards. John has only joined the Foundation today so he doesn't have a card linking him to the Foundation as yet. In the interim I'm approving John. Is there any more information you require from us?"

"No, thank you, I have all the contact details I require," said the detective.

As they walked away Emily said to John, "He thinks Roger is guilty. Roger might need surgery but we can visit him tomorrow morning." They walked back to Emily's car. She was exhausted and was anxious to get home. It had been a long day. Sitting in her car and gaining some strength, Emily pulled out her phone to let her parents know she would be coming home. There was a missed call from Ashley. She wished she could be open and honest with her. If Emily called now, she knew Ashley would sense a problem so she decided to speak with her tomorrow.

Emily sensed her new life path was more than just protecting the strangers; she had to protect her loved ones too. She knew Michael wasn't pure enough for Ashley and Emily would need to protect her as well. Saddened by the prospect that she wouldn't be able to spend as much time with Ashley as she always had in the past, Emily started the car ignition and drove back to Scarsdale.

Chapter Twenty-two

Emily felt completely exhausted from yesterday's revelations and Roger's incident that she crawled straight into bed and went straight to sleep. In the morning, she opened the doors to her balcony and stepped outside to enjoy the fresh morning air. It was a new day at the start of her new life. Her parents had made the right decision moving into the Newell estate. She looked over the secluded property and knew it was here that she would be able to be herself and develop and not have to hide.

Patricia and Martin were in the kitchen eating breakfast when Emily walked in.

"Good morning," they all said in unison.

"How was your night?" asked Patricia.

"Oh, nothing like I expected," answered Emily as she reached for a bowl. "We stumbled upon a crime scene. It involved a homeless man who had requested the Foundation's assistance." She relayed the details of the crime to her parents and explained Roger's close relationship to John. Patricia was happy that the Foundation could help him and Martin was happy to accommodate him at the hospital.

Emily noticed a shift in her father's mood. He seemed more subdued and not his normal cheerful self. "Dad, are you OK?" she gently asked.

"Of course I am. I didn't sleep well last night so I'm feeling a little tired."

"I'm heading to the hospital now. How about we meet later for lunch, just us?" she asked.

Martin agreed.

Emily walked outside to see John standing there. "I think it will be better to go together."

"You took a portal to Scarsdale for an immediate drive back into the city. You really don't need rest, do you?"

Chadi drove them both to the hospital. A police car was parked at the front. Nothing unusual, but Emily wondered if this police car was connected to Roger. Emily and John had just walked through the hospital main door, when Emily heard her name being called. John continued walking towards the lift, as Emily turned towards the person calling her name.

"Emily, wait up," yelled Michael.

"Hi Michael," said Emily. "How did you notice me?"

"I was just going to the Admin Office, when I saw you walk in. How have you been?"

"Good. How are you?"

"I was wondering," asked Michael, his face turning red. "I don't see you at the apartment very much and as Ashley and you're practically sisters. I was thinking that maybe we should all do dinner again soon."

Emily paused not wanting to hurt him, but she really wanted to spend her time with John now. "Sure," she said. "Why don't you get Ashley to organize it and I'll clear my schedule to be there. I have to go now as I have a client to meet, but it was nice seeing you again." But she didn't mean it.

"Yes, I heard you had taken on one of our patients. Have a wonderful day and I'll see you soon," said Michael, desperately.

Emily walked over to the reception desk. "Hi, I'm from the Foundation and I'm looking for Roger Lampoon's room. He was transferred last night."

"He's in room four-oh-two," replied the receptionist.

"Thank you. Do you know if his paperwork has been forwarded to the Foundation?" Emily flashed her Foundation ID.

"I was just about to fax a copy. Did you want to take it now?"

"Yes, thank you." Emily took the offered paperwork.

"Dr Lister was enquiring about Roger Lampoon as well. He also asked when you were due to come in, Miss Newell. He waited here a while. You must have just missed him because he's gone now," said the reception lady, looking around.

"Thank you," said Emily.

"That old boyfriend of yours still has a changing outline," said John as she approached. "I've never seen it before. He approached you as a blue outline and left as a yellow one. Something is very wrong with that man."

"Well, the meeting wasn't by chance. He'd been waiting for me."

Sitting outside Roger's room was a uniformed police officer. He was young and new to the job, which meant he was going to go by the book.

"Hi, my name is Emily Newell and I'm here to see Roger."

The officer opened his clipboard, "I'm sorry, Emily, you're not authorized to enter this room."

"My name is John Lawyer. Am I authorized?"

"Yes. Detective Major will be here soon to question him, so you won't have long," said the young officer.

"I'll go and sit in the waiting area," said Emily. "When the detective arrives, I'll ask him to add me to the list." Emily walked towards the lift as John entered the hospital room.

* * *

Roger lay motionless on the bed with a bandage covering his head and tubes running to his hand. He opened his eyes as John approached. "Hi Roger, how are you feeling?" asked John.

"Hi John, good to see you. What's with the suit?"

"New career," said John, smiling at his friend.

"How did you get past my police guard?"

"I'm now your Foundation lawyer."

Roger laughed, then sobered. "They think I killed someone. I would never do that."

John knew from Roger's outline that he wasn't capable of killing anyone. "I know. I thought it would be a misunderstanding."

"I'm enjoying the bed and food though. And the bathroom is clean and I can spend as long as I want in there."

"At least something good has come from this event," said John. "Roger, do you remember the attack?"

"They think I murdered the man that sleeps in your place at the fountain. I don't know. I can't remember. He was very quiet, kept mainly to himself. Do you remember the man that slashed Emily's arm?"

"Yes."

"He was there telling me he was after you, Emily and me. I was knocked out and when I came too I was the murder suspect," said Roger.

"The detective is on his way. Answer his questions but don't tell him what happened at the fountain before. That man is a very dangerous man," said John. "As your lawyer, I'm advising you to withhold that information until I can help you."

There was a knock on the door then Detective Major walked in. "Nice to see you awake, Roger. You're looking much better. I'd like to ask you some questions if you're up to it?"

"Yes, that's fine," said Roger looking at John for cues.

The detective read Roger his rights and then continued, recording the conversation under the permission of John.

"Roger, do you remember what happened last night?"

"Yes, parts of it."

"Did you act in self-defense?"

"The other man was sleeping next to me, someone else approached, mumbled something and then I passed out. My next memory is waking up and seeing the police," answered Roger.

"I'm sorry detective, but my client appears to be getting frustrated and tired. I think it would be better if you returned later, to give him time to recollect any further details," said John.

"John, I'll organize meetings with you," said Detective Major, shaking hands with John.

"Roger," he said, "rest up."

"Thank you," said Roger with no sincerity.

John followed the detective out and then walked towards the waiting area in search of Emily. He was concerned for her safety as well as Roger's.

"How is Roger?" asked Emily

"He told me that guy who slashed your arm was involved. He's after us as well. I've advised Roger to withhold the information on the man's identity until I figure out the motive and why we have now become targets. This has never happened before."

"What on earth does he want with me?" asked Emily. "That poor innocent man was helplessly murdered because of us. He thought that man was you, didn't he?" asked Emily.

"Let's get out of here. We need to continue our mission while searching for this man. He now believes I'm dead. I don't know if he will truly care to pursue you, but I'll be with you permanently. I must protect you."

"Why did he keep Roger alive?" asked Emily.

"I don't think he intended to. I don't think he realized that a homeless man could take a few knocks." He had reviewed Roger's medical file while he was talking to him. His injuries were deep and he would be staying in the hospital for another night before being moved to the prison. "Roger is being transferred to jail pending his court case. I'm sure the slasher will have contacts in the jail ready to kill him. I have the ability to place a protection over Roger. I'll need to return to his room. Do you want to wait for me here?"

"I'm meeting Dad for a coffee in the café. He couldn't make a lunch appointment. Can you please meet me there?"

John agreed and returned to Roger's room. "Roger, you have spent enough time with me to know I can do things. You have never betrayed me and I can help you now. When you go to jail, we're worried that people may try to kill you. Listen to what I say and again, never tell anyone. You must not change and turn bad. I can see you're still the same person and didn't commit this murder. We believe in you. You must not take advantage of the protection I am going to give you or you will lose it. People will ask you to be the leader in jail. If you say yes, you will have no protection. If you say no, we can defend you and restore your freedom. Once you're free, we can organize a job and a good life for you, do you understand?"

Roger nodded his head.

John held both of Roger's hands, looked him in the eyes and squeezed his hands tightly for about ten seconds. He then released them. "You must ignore what goes on around you. If someone hurts themselves, it was meant for you, but don't act like you know."

"Like the slasher with Emily?" asked Roger.

"Exactly."

"I don't know how to repay you," replied Roger. "Thank you, my friend. You've always taken care of me."

"I'm sorry to have you mixed up in this. After this is over you will be able to live in comfort. I promise you," said John. "I'm your lawyer, so you can request a visit from me when needed. They have my contact details, or Emily can contact me."

"Please thank Emily for paying my hospital bills. You wouldn't know the difference from this hospital to the last one. You are full of surprises. First my homeless friend and now my lawyer," smiled Roger, closing his eyes and suddenly falling asleep.

John left the room and walked back to the café. He didn't want to interrupt Emily and Martin so he sat out of view, watching them to ensure they were safe.

* * *

"Hi Dad," said Emily as her father stood up to hug her, "I'm so glad we could catch up."

"Me too," said Martin. "It's been a little busy lately. I appreciate our time."

"Dad, I just want you to know that no matter what I find out, no matter what my abilities are, my relationship and love for you will never change. I'll always try, like today, to have time with you and Mom. I promise."

* * *

John watched as Emily and John spent a few minutes together. He waited for Martin to leave before walking to Emily.

"How is Roger?" she asked.

"I've placed a protection on him," he said. John informed Emily about the protection transfer process and what the protection involved.

Emily loved hearing about all the possibilities before her.

"I made him go to sleep by speeding up the effect of the painkillers. He will start to feel better, but will not get a speedier transfer to jail. Knowing Roger, he will just enjoy the luxury of the hospital, free from pain. He knows not to focus on the protection. It can be misused with horrible consequences. He also said to thank you for paying his hospital bills."

"I'm glad he thought to call me," said Emily.

"When this is over, he would really like a job and a purpose."

"That is what the Foundation is for. We can help him to get set up, as long as he wants to help himself," said Emily.

Now Roger was safely asleep, they decided they would spend the rest of the afternoon walking around the streets to see what Emily could do. Now, more than any time before, she needed to discover her skills and perfect them. Practice was essential.

They walked out into the sunlight.

"Let's see what you can do," said John.

Chapter Twenty-three

The city was large and unpredictable. John and Emily walked without a destination in mind. John was dressed in his suit and Emily was in her work clothes; they both looked like an attractive couple.

Now John was all cleaned up, he appeared as a handsome man of approximately thirty-eight years. They were becoming friends and their easy familiarity showed. John didn't have a high emotional capacity yet, but Emily had planned some development training in the future. If she had to spend four hundred years with John, he would need more substance. She enjoyed the notion of training someone to be human.

"This activity is not about transferring consequence, but it's a learning lesson for you. However, if I notice an attack is being set up, I'll assist and detail it to you," explained John

"I know you're very experienced. It really does sadden me to hear you resign yourself to the inevitable." Emily was still very excited to be out in the street with a different focus. Usually she was assisting the homeless. With increased skills, she would be able to help the right people. She could not see colored outlines at present. However, the more she concentrated and focused on a person, the greater her insights would become and maybe one day she would be able to.

When John pointed out people with darker outlines, Emily was beginning to realize that what John was seeing, she was also feeling. Emily felt the intensity and weight of an evil person compared to the light-hearted joy of a good person. As they walked past people, Emily practiced by guessing the color outline based on her feelings.

They had walked to the outer edge of the city. "That person over there, I feel so heavy, he has got to be an orange outline," said Emily.

"Yes, he is. The person he is looking at, what color do you think she is?"

Emily concentrated on the woman. "Again, I feel so heavy. But surely that lovely looking woman is not orange?"

"Good, well bad, yes. She is orange and the two of them are waiting to set someone up. We could move on, but with two oranges, this may be a serious attack. Let's wait and watch." Emily and John walked over and sat down on a street bench close enough to watch. The orange couple didn't notice John or Emily, as they had already targeted their mark. Emily was in the middle of danger but didn't feel anxious. She now understood why John was keen to maintain his street patrols.

Walking towards the lovely looking lady was a man that Emily felt was perhaps a yellow outline. John confirmed it was.

"Hi," the orange lady said to the man as he was passing. "Do you have time to help me move a heavy piece of furniture? My apartment is very close by and it's hard without a man in my life."

The man was a nice person and whatever he thought the reward would be, he said, "Where's your apartment?"

"See that red brick building, half a block away, I live in there on the third floor."

He was suspicious. "Don't you have any neighbors who could help you?"

"No, they are too elderly. But don't worry, I'll wait and ask someone else," said the lady. "Thank you for stopping."

"OK, I'll help, but we must be quick," said the man.

"Thank you so much. Please follow me. It won't take long. What's your name?" asked the lady.

"My name's George and happy to help. What's your name?"

"Lola."

Emily and John listened and watched. Once George agreed to help, Lola's partner, who was waiting out of sight, walked off in the direction of the red brick building, but disappeared into a laneway just before it.

"See her partner?" said John. "He'll hide in the lane until Lola leads George past the entrance. Listen and you will hear Lola send a signal. Come on, we'll follow Lola. I can see the lane from here, but if he drags George in out of my sight, George may be seriously injured before I get there." Emily and John walked towards Lola and made sure John could see George.

As Lola and George walked past the lane entrance, Lola said, "Thank you, we're nearly there."

"Give us your wallet," said Lola's partner, brandishing a taser.

Lola stood beside the attacker.

"I thought your story was suspicious," said George. "I think it's disgusting to take advantage of kind souls and I'm not giving you my wallet."

The attacker lunged at him. "No worries, I'll get it myself." He tasered George with such force without any concerns for George's welfare. As expected, the attacker fell to the ground as the taser took effect. Lola and George looked at each other in shock.

When her partner stopped reacting to the taser, Lola picked it up. "Hand it over, George."

"Go your hardest, you disgust me," said George.

Lola turned up the taser with a stronger, longer charge and then she fell to the ground as the taser took effect.

"This is the strangest part, but I always have to do it," said John. "Run while you can," John yelled at George.

Emily remembered when John had called out to her after her arm got slashed. "We go into shock and need to be nudged out," said Emily as they watched George gather his senses and run away.

"Do you do anything with the two on the ground?" asked Emily.

"No, from experience I've noted they don't hang around for another target. They have no idea what happened and will still feel the effects for a while," said John. "What did you think about what you just saw?"

"It was bad, but just seems so fair. I can see why you like walking the streets. You don't inflict any violence; you just watch them do it to themselves."

"It's fulfilling but it's not something I would recommend for you to seek out. It can be a lonely existence and earth missions are loathed. Did you feel scared just now?" asked John.

"No, it was like watching a movie. Even if they came after us, I wouldn't be scared."

"Let's head out of this area and see if we can go back to identifying outlines. I think you're picking this skill up very quickly. This is starting to become my favorite earth mission," said John. "You just have to let your powers come through."

"I'm heading back to the apartment tonight. I think I need to help Ashley now that her and Michael are dating."

John said he was worried because he wasn't satisfied that Emily was able to protect herself against 'Slash' should he return. He wanted to place a protection over Emily but that would defeat the purpose of her training.

"John, the doors will be locked and you have a portal. I'll call you if there is anything to worry about," said Emily. "I need to be with Ashley tonight."

They walked back to Emily's apartment in silence. Emily was digesting the events, realizing that for her to learn these new skills, she would be witnessing acts of violence. She would now be subject to a world of evil.

"It's important that we have time for you to train too," said Emily, shocking John. He clearly didn't know he would also become the trainee. He said he saw and helped humans but he wasn't interested in becoming one.

When Emily walked into her apartment the television was on and Ashley was sitting comfortably in front of a movie.

"Hi Em," said Ashley, without turning around.

"Hi Ash. How are you?" Emily and Ashley had seen each other a week ago, but with the changes in Emily's life it felt like longer. They caught up with the details of each other's week, with Emily telling Ashley about the new lawyer at the Foundation. She withheld the details of why he was here.

"I saw Michael today," said Emily, opening up the subject with the intention of breaking them up.

"Yes, he told me," replied Ashley. "He said we need to organize a dinner together, maybe at your parents. He would love to see you all again."

Emily was shocked. That wasn't the dinner arrangement Michael had implied. "Oh OK. Are you interested in that?"

"It was a little unusual, but I love you all, so I was happy to go along with it."

"Ash," began Emily, treading softly. "Where is your relationship with Michael at?"

"Em, it's so complicated. Ryan is in Africa. I hurt him. Michael is a nice guy and I feel I should give him a chance out of respect for Ryan," replied Ashley.

Emily thought Ashley had never really loved Michael. She sensed Ashley was in love with the thought of Michael. He represented the life no one thought she was worthy of; the poor girl on a free ride had finally made it. Ashley was a doctor and now she was now a doctor dating a very handsome, high-profile doctor. Emily didn't want to say that to Ashley; the harsh truth could cause too much pain. Emily was sure Michael was using Ashley's vulnerability to manipulate her.

"Ryan is in Africa now. You sleeping with Michael didn't send him there. Ryan was going to leaving before that happened." Emily also sensed that Ashley was with Michael because she'd "traded" Ryan in for him.

"Em, it's complicated. You look so tired. How have you been?"

Emily made up a few boring and mundane events that had no need for questions. Emily and Ashley sat up together chatting, not going to bed until midnight. Emily told Ashley that for the next two weeks she would be staying in Scarsdale. Ashley didn't ask her why, assuming Michael was the cause.

Chapter Twenty-four

Emily's mind ran wild thinking of the adventures she would experience today. She avoided thinking about the attack and hoped hoped that with each new day she would develop a new skill. Emily and John agreed that John would visit Roger each day and Emily would spend human time however she chose because they didn't want to over-train her and cause her to lose focus. John had also reluctantly agreed to undergoing a full day of human training at least one day a week.

Emily had just finished breakfast when a soft beat filtered through her heart. "Morning John." She turned quickly to see him standing there.

"I waited for your friend to leave. She may have fainted seeing the homeless man, now dressed in a suit, appear out of nowhere."

"So where are we off to today?" asked Emily.

"I think we should head to the subway and see where we end up," replied John.

As they made their way towards the subway, they passed Michael sitting in a café. They waved and kept walking.

"He looks upset. Did your friend break up with him?" asked John.

"I doubt it. She would have messaged me if that was the case. I'm trying to make Ashley realize that Michael is not suitable for her. He didn't stay over last night, so I'm surprised he's in that café."

"Just tell her to break up with him. He's a bad person."

"John, that's not how it works. I'm so excited for our human training sessions. They can't come soon enough."

As they were approaching the subway, three young teenagers crossed the road. They were followed by a group of five. John spotted the potential danger before her. Emily felt the fear of the teenagers and the wild rage of the bigger group.

"John," Emily whispered. "An event like this would usually upset me, but I think your consequence transference is so fair, I really have no negative opinion." They watched the three teenagers enter the subway and the other group follow them. "Are they not safe in the subway?" asked Emily.

"No, and you'll probably find they'll be followed onto the train," replied John. "Come on."

John and Emily followed behind trying to go unnoticed. They didn't have time for Emily to use her Metro Card and John didn't need to. John held Emily's hand, and they both passed through the barrier.

"So much for deciding what to pay and where to get off," said Emily. "Will the cameras pick you up?"

"No. I don't appear on film. The photo ID card I showed at the hospital was just a card I needed rather than a card processed with a photo. As you said, I don't know where I'm going, so no ticket is the easier option," said John.

John and Emily walked down the platform and stood very close to the three anxious teenagers. The train pulled in and the teenagers entered the carriage with John and Emily behind. They sat next to the them on the train. Emily felt the teenagers were not dangerous but she wanted to confirm it with John.

"They all have the yellow outline. The large group are all orange," said John. As the doors began to close, the orange group entered the train coming over to stand in front of Emily, John and the teens in an intimidating way. There were three men and two girls. The three men stood in front.

"You're in our seats. You, your girlfriend and them will have to move," said one of the group members to John. He was obviously the leader.

"There are plenty of other seats and we're not moving." John put his hands in his pockets.

The man looked at Emily "He's a brave man, but it'll cost both of you now."

Emily smiled. "What is your problem?"

"No problem," he said, and threw a punch at John's face. The man stumbled back as he felt the force of the punch, feeling furious and thinking that John had hit him first. The next punch was harder and faster and, without knowing how, he was knocked to the floor bleeding. His friend went to his defense, and retaliation turned to fear when the second member suddenly lay knocked out on the train floor as well.

The two girls and remaining man stood in front of John and Emily screaming obscenities. One girl ripped at Emily's hair while the other girl scratched Emily across the face. Both girls screamed in pain and came back punching Emily's face. Emily was completely unhurt but felt sorry that the girls were so mean. The girls kept punching until they could not stand the pain anymore. They trembled and begged for the attack to stop, then sat down in the train seats, no longer watching or wanting to be a part of the attack.

The last man tried to kick John with such flexibility his leg kicked upwards. The leg didn't contact the man but the pain did. He stumbled back, returning with a punch so hard that it would have incapacitated a normal person. The man's fist turned on him and he fell to the ground.

John looked at the two quiet girls and then looked at Emily.

"What did you do?" he asked. "The girls' outlines are flashing between orange and blue."

Emily could see they were terrified and confused. Emily touched their hands. "Ladies, today you have been given a choice. You can continue on this path of destruction or you can have a meaningful life. Fate is in your hands and you now have a clear direction to help you choose."

"What happened?" asked John.

Emily was confused as well; this was new to her too. As a psychologist, she could see the girls pain and knew they needed guidance. Emily's touch had cleared their minds. Changing their life direction wouldn't be as hard as they had originally thought. Emily gave the girls clarity; the choice was theirs. They were no longer trapped. Emily knew, without knowing how, that she could only offer this opportunity once per person. She hoped the girls would seek a better life.

John normally walked away from the attack unnoticed, but Emily wanted to assess the boys to make sure they were OK. Emily questioned the boys, making sure she didn't say anything incriminating.

"Thanks for your help," said the red-haired teenager. "Maybe I should learn self-defense before chatting up another girl."

"That won't help you. These people outnumbered you," replied John, before thinking.

Several other passengers scattered throughout the carriage had called the police. The two girls exited the train at the next stop. John and Emily also exited the train at the same stop as they didn't want to be questioned by the police.

"Do you ever call the police?" she asked.

"No. I never draw attention to myself. No one will be able to describe me, you or what really happened. When the three men get back together, the fight sequence will be very vague in their memories and they'll only know the three teenagers were able to look after themselves."

"What about the Roger event then? How did the man who attacked me remember you?"

"He had noticed me before he had noticed you, and so in his sequence of events I was involved. He could have assumed I'd attacked him. Also, he was looking for me because of his boss. But enough of that. I need to understand what happened with those two girls. They left without acknowledging either of us or their friends. Their outlines were flashing blue-orange before your touch and after they were flashing yellow-blue. Emily, none of us have the power to change an outline. I've never seen an orange change to a blue. I need to test you again. I need you to transfer the next consequence on your own," said John.

"Are you saying that you're afraid of what happened?" asked Emily, disappointed that John hadn't praised her for the obvious progress in her abilities.

"Emily, you transferred the consequence. It was perfect and more than I expected from you in a day's worth of training. Your transfer included an emotional transfer. We need to understand all your skills. This is a very different mission and we're both learning."

"That was such a rush! I can't believe I was able to do that!"

"I'll never understand you humans," said John.

"Yes, you will," replied Emily. "You know, I think when I was growing up it was a case of suppressing my powers as I didn't realize what they were. There was a time when Ashley and I were hiking. We were about thirteen years old. Ashley had fallen and it warranted a break or a sprain but she stood up unharmed. I had felt her fear as she fell and must have done something. We were both shocked that she walked away unharmed."

"That is not a transfer for consequence." John looked confused. "That sounds like a protection. It differs from my form of protection where I give people some of my powers."

"I genuinely think I helped. I just needed you to help me," said Emily.

"It's probable. We could push Ashley down and see if she's unhurt. But I'm sure Ashley wouldn't appreciated that."

Emily laughed. *He doesn't even realize he's being funny. I'm going to enjoy training John,* thought Emily. "John, there is one more important task I want to learn. Can we return to the Foundation through the portal? I deserve to enjoy the perks."

John said he wasn't sure of the amount of air inside the portal and if it could be harmful to Emily. "It's a relatively small distance. You may need to hold your breath for a short amount of time. As long as you don't panic, it will be a good opportunity to test how you travel. I create a portal and walk through, so it will be the same, but you will need to walk behind me and keep both hands on my shoulders. Check to see if you can see me rather than just feel me. I'm not sure if I'll be able to find you should you ever let go."

"Will I be alright?" asked Emily.

"Keep your hands on me at all times and keep your eyes open," said John.

Emily walked around him nervously. John's reservations had Emily doubting if it was such a clever idea. She stood behind and held on to his shoulders. "Ready," said Emily, her grip tightening even more.

"We'll take about two steps and then be in the portal. Stay close and keep pace with me."

Emily was aware of nothingness and then she was standing outside the Foundation. John was with her and her hands were still on his shoulders. She laughed as she looked around. "Wow!" A thrill ran through her. "This new world is so exhilarating!"

"That seemed quick and I wasn't aware of any oxygen issues. How long did it take us to travel?" Emily removed her hands from John's shoulders.

"The travel is timeless so we have arrived here at the same time as we entered the portal," said John.

"Is it like that when you travel home?"

"There is a designated portal that I must go to and enter, rather than just create the mini portals for travel around here. As soon as I enter the portal to go home, I'm automatically gone one week of your time. Depending how long I stay with my father, depends on the total time I'm away," answered John. "I know why you're asking and it's too soon to even consider taking you over there yet."

"All in good time," said Emily.

"It's not a simple matter of just taking you there. We don't know if you would survive. We don't rely on the same necessities as you such as air and water."

Being outside the Foundation and back to reality reminded Emily of her job. She didn't want to neglect her clients so she planned on going to work to catch up on files.

"John, I'm having dinner with my parents tonight, and you're welcome to join us. Then we can go through the portal again. It really is the only way to travel."

"Thank you, I won't be joining you. I don't need food to survive. I'll collect you at eight tonight and we can walk around, then portal back to Scarsdale." John smiled at Emily, walked a few steps and was gone.

Too funny, thought Emily. *I've not even walked into my office and John is probably already in the city.* Emily entered the Foundation and walked over to the water cooler, gulping down cup after cup of water. She was surprised by how thirsty she was. *I must remember to drink more water when I'm with John,* she thought. Emily had only known about her Purifier side for several days, but it felt like a lifetime. Learning of the life was a shock but understanding it was a thrill. The next few weeks her training would intensify and training John would take up a lot of her time. She made an appointment with Patricia to move her workload at the Foundation.

"How was your morning?" asked Patricia.

"It's been so interesting. It's rewarding to protect innocent people and to see the attackers attack themselves. But it's difficult to watch the evils of mankind," Emily said.

"It sounds like a challenging world is ahead of you."

"It will take some physical and emotional training on my part. I'm hoping by training John, we can help each. There is a major perk to this life. I could use the portal after all. John helped me, but I had to hold on to him. Mom, as you blink, I could be in Scarsdale."

"Emily, I always knew you were special, I just never knew how special. There is only one Emily on this planet. I always knew you were here to leave a mark on this world," said Patricia, proudly.

After a quick conversation about the files, Emily returned to her office and completed her workload for the day.

* * *

As organized, she met her parents for dinner. Emily was very hungry, having not eaten since breakfast. Conversation soon turned to Michael.

"Michael, via Ashley, asked to have dinner with us all. He thought the estate would be a nice place," said Emily, rolling her eyes.

"For Ashley's sake, of course we will. We're free this Sunday if they are open for the invitation. Please extend the invite to John. He's now permanently part of our family and we want him to feel welcomed," said Martin.

Tonight's dinner turned out to be quick and customary. The news had not changed the family dynamic. Martin and Patricia felt part of the journey just as much as Emily. She had not excluded them. She had hoped to include Ashley in the journey, but that detail was determined by John, not Emily.

When they left the restaurant, John was outside waiting. He spent a few minutes talking to Patricia and Martin. Meanwhile, Emily called Ashley to confirm the details of the dinner date. The conversation was brief but not out of the ordinary. Emily felt good chatting with her.

"So, Michael tells me he has seen you a few times with a new man. A new boyfriend?" asked Ashley.

Emily laughed. "It's the lawyer I told you about from the Foundation. He's taken on a major case that involves the police. You'll recognize him as the homeless man from the car accident. All I can say is that I've been working with him and now he has returned to his career," said Emily. "I have to go, Ash. I'll speak to you soon. Remember to confirm Sunday with Michael."

"Thank you," said Ashley, not referring to the specific dinner date arrangement. Emily felt it was a subtle thank you for Emily's understanding and support with Michael. She thanked her parents for dinner and said goodbye. Patricia and Martin walked to their car and John and Emily walked around the corner.

Chapter Twenty-five

Emily and John exited the portal. "Isn't this the better part of the city?" Emily asked.

"Usually it is, but at this time of the week all the areas seem to experience the same amount of crime," answered John.

"The man over there, sitting on the street bench looking at the store." Emily pointed at an obvious drug addict. "Is he responsible for his actions?"

"Why should someone else be hurt? He'll do the action therefore he'll get the consequence."

They watched as the addicted man walked towards the store. He moved something from his back pocket to his front pocket before entering.

"You can't see him. Aren't we going to follow?" asked Emily in a very anxious tone.

"Did you not see the homeless man follow him into the store?"

"Is there another one like you here?"

"We weren't too sure how much time it would take to help you. He's here on a quick mission and will probably go back in another two weeks," said John.

A scream came from inside the shop. They turned to see the drug addict stumble out covered in blood. He fell to the ground as John walked towards him. The homeless man exited the shop and walked away as John would have done previously.

"You're hurt. I can see you're not a bad person," John bent down and reached for one of the man's hands. "Do you want to be free of your addiction?"

"Are you insane? I'm hurt and need an ambulance!" the drug addict yelled, impatiently.

"I can help you if you want to be sober," said John.

"It is what it is. An ambulance is what I need now," said the man.

"OK," said John releasing the man's hand and standing up.

"Are you calling an ambulance?" asked Emily.

"You know I don't get involved. He wants to stay the way he is, so his life is not going to get better anytime soon. Someone will call an ambulance. We'll wait to make sure no one is injured in the meantime." Emily reached for her phone, but John stopped her. "You cannot make the call. If you are to call for an ambulance every time this happens, people will begin to ask questions. It's not plausible for anyone to be at nearly every crime scene."

Emily placed the phone back in her bag, "This will be difficult. I understand your reasoning, but it pains me to not be able to help. This man is influenced by a drug."

"A drug taken by choice," said John. "I don't understand your conflict. This man chose this life. Why should it pain you? This is all part of your training."

"And part of yours," replied Emily.

The homeless man approached John and Emily. The three walked over to a street bench across the road. Each sat down so they could view the drug addict and wait for the ambulance.

John sat in between Emily and the homeless man. John turned to Emily. "This is John. He's the one who saved the shop owner from the attack."

The homeless John nodded at lawyer John, faced Emily, nodded again and smiled. He must have been new; he made her John's social skills look perfect.

"Hi John," said Emily. Emily looked at lawyer John and asked, "Is everyone named John?"

"You need names and so we give you one. Everyone who comes here is called John."

"It's nice you all know how to smile. Don't know if you get the emotional impact, but the facial movement is obviously in your body training," said Emily. "One more question. Why did my heart not skip a beat when I met this John? Is my connection only with you?"

Lawyer John looked at the homeless John. "Do you feel any connection to Emily?"

"No, just with you," he said.

"What connection do you feel with me?"

"I know we're from the same place."

John the lawyer turned back to look at Emily. "I don't know why we feel the connection. I'm sure we'll find out the reason when the King has finished his investigation into your birth."

"You just file all this information for later. Your lack of concern separates you from me," said Emily, feeling disturbed that most of her questions were still going unanswered.

"Yes," replied John the lawyer.

Emily smiled, amused by John's innocence. She understood that John didn't have the answers, but it wasn't humanely possible for Emily not to seek immediate answers of her existence.

The drug addict was still lying on the footpath. He was bleeding and moaning. A lady walking by stopped to help. She bent down and kneeled on her, trying to work out how to help him. The addict pulled out his knife. The trio watched the scenario unfold.

The addict slashed at the woman's thigh with his other hand positioned to snatch her bag as the lady reacted in pain. The lady saw the knife attack, heard his scream of pain and reacted in disgust.

"I'm the one who stopped to help you and you attack me?" she asked.

"I need money for my next hit. I've been stabbed twice and need an ambulance. I've no idea what's going on." The wounded addict was bleeding from two savage wounds. It was obvious he'd experienced deep impact with each stab wound and was now feeling the full brunt of his actions.

John the lawyer walked over to the lady on the footpath. "Can you please call an ambulance and then just walk away?"

"He tried to attack me," said the lady, more in shock than anything else.

"You've tried to help and he's betrayed you. Don't try to work him out. Tell the ambulance to contact the police and they'll take care of him. You've been more than helpful and that shop owner, over there in that store, will have a story for the police as well." John pointed to the relevant store.

"Thank you, I really had no idea what to do." The lady made the phone call and walked over to the street bench facing the store to wait for the police. She ignored the bleeding man's pleas for help and even stopped another man from offering any assistance.

John walked back sit next to Emily; the homeless John had already left and was back at work. "Emily, I want to test something, I don't know if my theory is plausible but please come with me to the addict and stand above him. I'm hoping he'll try to attack you."

Emily took a few moments digesting a statement that a week ago would have seemed crazy. The sound of emergency vehicles in the distance was growing louder with each second.

"Oh no, the moment has been missed," said John.

The lady approached the police and gave them her story. She then pointed to the store and Emily and John watched as one policeman went into the store and the other walked over to stand near the bleeding man on the street. The ambulance arrived and the man was loaded in and left with a police escort. John and Emily had stayed for the police to tend to the bleeding man. Once the man was gone, the danger was gone and they were now happy to be free to move on.

"I could tell he didn't want to change and so didn't waste time trying to make him sober, only to have him resume his addiction," explained John to Emily's unasked question.

"That is the skill I really want to develop. You have no idea how frustrating it's to try and help some of our clients only to realize they had no intention of taking advantage of the help being offered," said Emily. "I'll be holding hands a lot more. I'm laughing just thinking about the reaction I'll be getting." John returned the laugh. This made Emily laugh even more.

He looked as surprised by this new act of feeling as she was. "This mission is certainly different."

Emily was happy with her subtle training of John. They walked towards a group of people. John could see their motives and Emily could feel them. Neither of them had to tell the other what they thought. The group surrounded two businesswomen who looked like they had been for after-work drinks. The group took the women's wallets, phones and tablets. The women were frightened, but were not hurt. The group walked away.

"The women probably think the robbery was their fault!" said Emily.

"We don't understand it. You humans have a way of blaming yourselves for other people's faults" answered John.

"What happens now?"

"The group is just around the corner, waiting for their next target. They didn't hurt anyone. They used their numbers to intimidate the two women, so there is no consequence."

"Really?"

"We can create a possible consequence, if you like," replied John.

"Yes, please. I must help the homeless so it's too unfair to allow these people to make life so hard for others. What can I do?"

"You have seen that they try to intimidate others. I'll leave you alone so all you have to do is become a target and resist. If they attack you, they'll receive their consequence. If they don't attack you, then we move on," said John.

"OK, but don't go too far." Emily pulled out her cell phone and prepared to make a call. She walked around the corner, saw the group and kept walking past them. They surrounded her and demanded her phone and bag. Emily acted surprised. "Sorry, I'd be lost without my phone. You can't have it." One man made a grab for the phone, but Emily was quicker and put her phone into her bag.

"Give me your bag," screamed one of the men.

"I've said no! Let me past, I'm already late." Emily started to walk towards the opening in the group.

"Grab her! Hold her arms," called one to the other.

Emily was grabbed from behind. Another man came up close to Emily's face. "You need to learn respect," he said.

"Obviously not from you," said Emily.

The man was infuriated and swung a punch at her face. The punch wasn't hard enough to knock the man down, but would have made a woman unconscious. The man threw two more punches in quick succession then fell to the ground. The remainder of the group all jumped in to attack Emily. Emily's arms were still held behind her back to assist others with the attack.

One by one, the group members attacked Emily and each ended up on the ground. The attacking men took a lot more punches to knock themselves out while trying to hit her than when they were hitting John. She realized she must be trying to save them some pain.

The man behind Emily had been twisting Emily's arms further and further up her back, until he could no longer stand the pain he was inflicting on himself. He let go and pushed Emily by her head hard towards the sidewalk. He knocked himself out after three attempts and Emily found she was the only one left standing.

John walked over with the two women that had just been robbed. "Thank you for trusting me. Ladies, if you would like to get your items back, please help yourself."

The women took their items back, thanking Emily for standing up to the group. The two women walked quickly away and this time they didn't feel they deserved to be robbed. "They got what they deserved," said one woman to the other. "Good lesson for us," replied the other as they walked away.

"John, did you notice I was trying to save my attacker some pain and the attack took longer to end?" asked Emily.

"That is what was different when I saw you get your arm slashed. He grabbed his heart through your pain, and his cut on the arm wasn't as deep as he tried to inflict on you."

Emily walked over to the man sitting alone and injured. "What is wrong with you?"

"I'm sorry, I don't want this. I don't want to hurt anyone," the man replied.

Emily helped him up, off the ground. "You now have a choice about the person you want to become. Today is a new day. You have one chance to pick a more rewarding path. I hope you take it."

"You have no idea how remarkable you are," said John, proud of his trainee. "Emily, this group all had orange outlines. As you know, I cannot help a person with an orange outline. But the man you touched is now blinking a blue outline. Emily that was you! You transferred the consequence and somehow, I don't know how, gave this man an opportunity to better himself. I'll need to monitor this man. I need to understand how long it lasts and what, if anything, will happen to break it."

"But why just him?" asked Emily. "He was the only man to speak to me."

"You both looked at each other. I think it was at this point that you were able to help him. How, I don't know. But again, this is just my theory," replied John.

Emily and John walked away leaving the group lying on the sidewalk. As they walked along the streets many people approached them and asked, "Any spare change?"

Emily gave vouchers to the genuine needy and just said no to the opportunists.

"I don't understand why so many people keep asking," said John.

"They know that people will always help another person if they can. The people asking for change really do receive money just by asking. It's a win/win for everyone. Those who can afford it will always help those who need it. We think of it as doing a good turn, so we can enjoy a good turn," explained Emily.

John and Emily continued to walk along the streets and were approached to be robbed as well. While the scenario was with different people, the outcome was always the same. After one of the robbers was left lying on the sidewalk, John and Emily continued their walk.

"I'm surprised to be noticed by so many people," said John. "As a homeless man I'm never seen, yet while wearing a suit it's completely different."

While Emily and John continued to walk around the streets for another hour, they saw many attempted assaults. Emily thought watching the carjacking was very surreal. A car stopped and a man approached to check the door handles. The driver's door was unlocked, so the carjacker opened it and placed a gun at the driver's head. The carjacker pulled the driver out of the car and attempted to throw him onto the road into the oncoming traffic. When the driver should have fallen on the road, it was the carjacker that was thrown into the oncoming traffic.

The driver was still sitting in his car. The door was open and he was watching everything in deep shock. Emily helped him to steer the car into the curb where John joined her. "Would you like us to sit with you until you get over the shock?" asked Emily.

"Do you have any idea what just happened?" asked the driver.

"No, it happened too fast. But you may need to talk to us for a couple of minutes to get over the shock," said Emily.

"Thank you. I do need to calm down before driving home." John got into the front passenger seat and Emily got into the back seat. They all watched the ambulance arrive and take the man from the street to the hospital.

"Thank you for staying with me. I feel OK now to continue," said the driver after another ten or so minutes.

"You're welcome. Good night and remember to lock your car doors," said Emily. They watched the car drive down the street and away into the night. "John, I know we could stay here all night helping people, but I'm really tired so I'll have to go home."

"All right, it's getting late. I'll take you to your home, just near the front door so not to disturb your parents. I'll walk you out, you let go of my shoulders and I'll turn and walk straight back into the portal," said John.

"I'll be surprised if anyone is still awake, but streamlining our travel is good. I love the portal and whatever you want is OK with me," said Emily. *John has no idea of the New York traffic and I'm so enjoying my absence from it,* thought Emily to her tired self.

"Just before we end tonight, I want you to know how much I appreciate what you are doing for me. I know this is your mission but you don't make me feel like I'm only a mission," said Emily. "I would like to repay you. Perhaps take you to a Broadway show and show you some of New York's tourist attractions – maybe even a nightclub with dancing. I'll get the tickets and ease you into that side of things. This is a great city in a great world and with you now in my life for a very long time, you may appreciate witnessing some kindness, love and even fun."

"I know tonight has been a shock for you and this is why we don't stay here long. We help where we can and do leave with a sense of appreciation for our own society. I'll be with you for a long time. So if that means I have to stay here for a long time, then I guess you are right. It will be beneficial to see the good side of your life. Yes, I'll go with you and the other John can cover the streets for a while. I can get the tickets if you like," said John.

"Great! I know you can pull tickets out of your pocket. However, I'm happy to buy them and let you know when we're going."

"OK. Are you ready to go home now?"

"Yes, please," answered Emily.

John turned his back and Emily placed her hands on his shoulders. They took two steps and, just as quickly, another two steps into Emily's front home foyer.

Emily lowered her hands from John's shoulders, said "See you," and watched John turn and disappear.

"If I didn't have Chadi, I would be so jealous of your travel," said Martin.

"Dad, how come you're still up?"

"I woke up and realized I had left my phone downstairs. I was just getting it to take back upstairs," replied Martin. "I can see why you would love to travel via the portal."

"I'm so spoilt, I can't imagine travelling any other way now."

"Is there any way you can walk out and bump into people walking by?"

"John said he can control his exits and walks out only when it's clear."

"Goodnight, Emily. I know it's been another long day for you," said Martin walking towards the staircase.

"It's been a very long and very interesting day. Goodnight, Dad," said Emily, following him up the stairs.

Chapter Twenty-six

Martin and John sat in the Newell sitting room. "Emily is determined to balance your life and her own. I understand she is taking you out to a club tonight," said Martin.

"Martin, I really appreciate all the time you have taken with me. It's really different to look for the good, rather than transfer the bad," said John, "I must say, I've been inside many clubs and I wouldn't say they are the best places to find good."

"Sometimes you need to focus on the positive and push aside the negative. Try to remember that where there is bad, there is also good. You don't want to lose sight of the people who matter. You are part of our family now; we don't consider you as our mission. I love Emily so much and want to give you both a very strong foundation for such a long life together. I thank you for all the time you have spent with me explaining what is ahead of you," said Martin.

"Thank you," replied John. "Am I dressed OK for a club?

"Most people wear casual clothes. Although, in a suit, you're dressed OK and will fit ..." Martin stopped as John morphed into casual attire. "Right, arh, OK, that is exactly what I was thinking. Emily has organized Chadi to drive so you get to feel the initial excitement and anticipation. We know you won't yet, but in time you may. At the nightclub, you can dance, laugh and just have a really fun time. Do you know how to dance?"

"I'm not sure what this body can do. I'll watch and when Emily points out a good dancer, I'll just follow their actions," replied John.

"Be discreet. If he sees you copying his moves he may think you're making fun of him. Try to copy a lot of people and just mix the dance moves together."

John nodded.

"I'm sure Emily will get you to try an alcoholic drink and once again, you'll be able to experience another body change."

"I know Emily has her own mission. But she's also very aware of my lack of human experience so I trust her," said John.

Emily looked beautiful as she walked down the staircase to meet John.

"You look so handsome," said Emily.

"Great shirt, shame the color isn't darker," said Emily as the color began to darken on John's shirt.

"That's another skill I really want!" said Emily.

* * *

After the portal, the drive to the club felt long even though there was no traffic chaos. Chadi dropped them at the venue. The beat of the music could be heard as they stood in line. The night air was invigorating, encouraging people to venture inside.

"Are you alright?" asked John.

"It's OK. The wind is just a little too refreshing for what I'm wearing." A cool chill swept over Emily causing her to shiver.

John was looking at the people standing in line. "You have chosen wisely. Not an orange outline in sight … so far."

"It's one of the finest clubs in the state. I wanted to minimize the evil, not that that is always possible."

"Well Emily, so far so good."

Emily and John had made their way to the front of the line when a group of men in black suits entered the club before them. No one needed Purifier abilities to know that these men were either owners of the establishment or knew the owners.

Emily turned to John. "So?"

"All orange," replied John.

"I've been here on numerous occasions and nothing has ever happened," said Emily.

John knew Emily wanted him to experience the world; to see it for its beauty not for its horror. "I'll ignore the orange outlines this time," said John. The suited men walked towards a private area. "An orange person probably has some time off as well …"

The music grew louder as they made their way through the crowd and to the bar. John scanned the room. He was impressed with the social gathering: mostly yellow outlines, a few whites and a few blue. There was no one else for John to be concerned about.

"What would you like to drink?" asked Emily. "Have you tried alcohol before?"

"No I haven't. I've heard about it and I've seen it alter a person's outline. I'm not sure what the effects may be."

"How about a sip before I order you one for yourself?" Emily faced the barman. "One Long Island Ice Tea please."

John stepped back from the bar and continued to scan the room, taking in the social event. The bar was lit with purple lighting, complemented by strong orange lighting over the shelves of alcohol bottles. The remainder of the room was blue. The left of the front entrance had walls lined with white leather lounges, the right section was filled with comfortable tub chairs and tables. In the center of the large room was a dance floor and in front was the impressive bar which was now crowded.

"Come on John, let's find a place to sit," said Emily. John followed Emily as she ventured into the crowd and made her way over to two tub chairs alongside two women. "May we join you?" asked Emily.

"Sure," replied one of the girls.

John stared at them intently as he sat down. John noticed Emily's disapproving expression and could feel her sense of uneasiness.

"You cannot just stare at people like that," whispered Emily.

"I've never been in a place like this before. I was distracted and with the loud music around me I didn't know what to do. It's a lot different to sitting with Roger at the fountain," replied John.

"So, John, would you like a sip?"

"I guess for the first time on this planet I'm having a night off," said John, taking the drink.

Emily laughed. "Welcome to the real world."

John took a sip and coughed, "You call that a beverage?" He reached for the bottle of water.

"It gets better as the night goes on." Emily ordered John his own alcoholic drink, and then another. John wasn't getting drunk. He was just enjoying the changes it made to his mission.

"Would you like to dance?" asked Emily.

"Can you point to a man that is dancing well so I can see what is expected?"

Emily laughed, looked around and pointed to a man in a blue shirt. John looked at the man for a few minutes. "Ready," he said. "I've never danced before." As they walked onto the dance floor, John took Emily's hand as he had seen other men do.

Emily started to dance while John attempted to imitated the man in the same blue shirt John now wore. "Just let the beat of the music take control of your body," said Emily. "And, you don't need to wear the same shirt."

John began to move in rhythm to the beat. "Like this?" he asked.

"You're a natural. Is there anything you can't do?"

John and Emily stayed on the dance floor for several songs. They were both enjoying having such a great time when a young man brushed up against John. The man was approaching a couple.

"Hey!" shouted the young man approaching the couple. "That's my woman."

The young lady tried to stop the approaching, aggressive man. "Nick, stop! He didn't know."

"I'm sorry, I didn't know she was with you."

Nick threw a heavy punch and immediately fell to the ground with a bleeding nose. It happened so fast, his girlfriend and the young man had no time to react or understand what had happened. Patrons began to gather as the fight started. Instead of looking who had blindsided him, Nick staggered as he stood up, wiping the blood from his nose with his hand. "I don't know who hit me, but you'll pay for that!" Nick swung another punch, this time to the man's jaw. Nick moaned as he lay on the floor, semi-conscious. Security had walked over once they saw the crowd form a circle. They had watched the fight and were perplexed that one man was the aggressor and the victim.

"Step outside," said Security to the young women and the two young men. A security guard helped Nick up off the floor and lead them all from the establishment.

John and Emily went and sat back down in the chairs. "Why did you intercept that? It was a simple argument between two young men," asked Emily, confused that John would intervene in a simple fight.

"Nick is an orange outline and although he wouldn't be able to critically injure that young man in here, he would have waited for him outside. If he had punched that man in the face the first time, Security would have forced all three to leave the premises, giving Nick access to the young man. The young lady intentionally instigated the fight. She enticed that young man for her own self-gratification knowing that Nick would come to her rescue. She also has an orange outline," said John.

"So, is the young man OK out there?"

"Yes, he'll be fine. Nick will need medical treatment and the woman will portray the heartbroken girlfriend while the young man will have time to leave unnoticed. I noticed his friends followed him out of the club." John looked at Emily and smiled. It was the one emotion he had discovered since meeting Emily. "Please don't let this event upset you. I've had a wonderful night. How about another dance?"

Emily and John walked onto the dance floor.

* * *

Looking out, from a private room hidden from public view were the men in suits who had cut the line in the club. The scene between Nick and the young man had made them look over. They were now watching Emily and John intently.

"That's them," said a different man. As he reached for his glass of whisky, he exposed the slash on his arm. "He's still alive."

* * *

John and Emily left the club and walked into the chilly night air. Emily shivered and John handed her a coat to put on.

"Where did this come from?" asked Emily.

"You were cold so I got you a coat." They walked around the corner and into a portal. Emily was again delivered inside her front door.

"John, I enjoyed tonight with you trying out different emotional lessons. Can you meet me here tomorrow at ten o'clock? I want to take you to another place for you to test your body and investigate more emotions."

"I trust you Emily, and this does sound important. Are we going to a research testing lab?"

"You could call it that – or an amusement park – whichever you prefer is fine with me." Emily laughed. "I hope the alcohol doesn't affect you tonight and tomorrow. Thanks John and goodnight."

* * *

The next morning John and Emily were first in line when the amusement park opened. There were no crowds so Emily hoped it would be a fun, relaxing time. Emily took John on the rollercoaster first. They sat in the front seat and John watched with interest as the train climbed slowly up the steep slope. When they reached the top, John was surprised to feel the speed greatly increase as it plummeted down the steep drop. The train continued to go very fast and John felt his stomach jerk while his physical body was jolted in all directions. He looked at Emily who was screaming, laughing and watching him. The ride ended very quickly and John found he needed a few seconds to step out of the carriage.

"Well," said Emily. "What emotions did you feel then?"

"What did you feel? I'm not sure what I was meant to feel," answered John.

"OK. That was the first ride. I felt excitement, freedom, joy, anxiety and perhaps a taste of the alcohol from last night." Emily asked John to choose the next ride.

He watched the rides to work out the emotional level and decided on the drop ride. He and Emily were locked onto their seat as the ride took them slowly up to a great height. They were expecting to be dropped so they were anticipating and preparing for the drop. The ride left them sitting for an extended time and then dropped without warning.

This time John felt the anticipation and excitement of the ride and had a very big smile on his face. They stayed at the park for two hours. The queues started to get longer and John also learnt patience and to wait his turn. Each ride provided excitement and a thrilling outcome. John did like this testing lab and was happy when Emily laughed through most of the tests, even if he didn't have those reactions.

John realized that getting to know the working of his human body would help him to understand Emily and her needs on a deeper level.

Chapter Twenty-seven

The last two weeks had been very busy and productive. John had been refining Emily's skills and attending to Roger's case. For the first time on Earth, John was rushed off his feet and Emily needed to add multi-tasking to his lesson plan. John was also helping more at the Foundation. He had helped Ashley set up her new drug rehabilitation program. Ashley was responsible for screening the applicants but John used his magic to ensure they accepted the right applicants. Emily enjoyed spending time with John, learning and developing her skills. She was preparing for a long future with John by balancing both of their lives with work and fun.

John and Emily still walked many kilometers. On one of their morning runs, Emily noticed John had slowed his pace to get behind her. She turned around and John was nowhere to be seen. He had used a portal to meet her at the end of the run. Emily laughed and was delighted by John's progress. He was beginning to act like a human and they were becoming close friends.

Emily loved her sport and outdoor life and wanted John to value these activities. They played a game of golf together, but after the second hole Emily had to ask John not to use his

Purifier skills as, otherwise, there would be no point to the game. Playing a game of golf with an opponent who continually got a hole in one was very demoralizing and lacked challenge. Watching John struggle with the hitting concept was much more fun. John quickly learnt the emotions of frustration and anger.

Emily had taken John out to a Broadway show. After he learnt they were acting a story, he sat back and relaxed. He could guess the story outcome but didn't realize you don't tell the ending before it happens, so Emily had to teach him secrecy.

At each venue, Emily found that she had to keep moving his focus from the impending trouble to the fun side of life. Emily realized if you are always on the look-out for trouble you can easily find it. Her "mission" was to get John to relax. Her first goal was for John to experience as many emotions as possible and try to get in touch with his human body. Both John and Emily worked hard on their lessons and respected each other's intentions. While Emily enjoyed spending so much time with John, she missed Ashley terribly.

Ashley was inundated with her residency, the Foundation projects and her relationship with Michael. When Emily was at the Foundation she would take the opportunity to catch up and chat with Ashley. Emily still needed to eat, clean and sleep, so she tried to take advantage of this time to be with her loved ones. She still shared her life between the apartment and the estate. She preferred the estate as she hated lying to Ashley and equally hated seeing Michael.

It was finally the night of the family dinner that had been scheduled with Michael. The date had been changed twice to fit in with differing schedules so everyone was happy to finally get it over with. With Michael continually reminding Emily and Ashley about this dinner, Emily allowed herself a smile, as she thought about the family dinner with Michael's family. *So happy it's in the past and nothing to do with my future,* thought Emily.

She remembered the stress prior and during the Lister family dinner. *Poor Ash!*

Emily helped Patricia prepare the meal and now she helped to set the table for dinner. "It'll be nice to have Ashley here for dinner. I miss her. This'll be the first time Michael will be able to speak to John. It should be interesting; I just hope it's not awkward."

Patricia nodded and passed a plate.

"John sees a blue outline so I've told him to not stare at Michael like he would on the street. I told him tonight was the test to see how far he had developed as a human, not for work."

"I know you tried to talk Martin out of inviting John, but he really only has your best interest at heart. Plus, John is family now. Your dad wouldn't be comfortable excluding him," said Patricia.

"I just feel Michael's motives for this dinner are not genuine."

"I think we all feel that," replied Patricia, "but Ashley is like another daughter, so we'll do this for her."

"That's why am I helping her. I don't want her with Michael."

"Well Em, sometimes a friend just needs to be supportive and stand beside them."

John arrived an hour before Ashley and Michael. Emily laughed thinking they would have all left Manhattan at the same time, with John arriving before they had the chance to turn on the car ignition. Dinner was planned for seven o'clock. At six thirty the front gate intercom sounded.

* * *

Ashley had a key to the house, but Michael insisted on knocking at the front door. He was expected to knock at his mother's house, so he thought Ashley was exceptionally rude for even thinking of entering the house unannounced.

They all greeted Ashley as they would on any other day; she was part of the family.

"Welcome back, Michael," said Martin, walking to shake his hand. Michael stepped in and kissed Patricia on the cheek. Michael noticed John, standing beside Martin. He tried unsuccessfully to control his displeasure.

"Michael, this is John. He'll be joining us tonight," said Martin.

Michael was fuming about John's presence. He waved to Emily as opposed to greeting her warmly like he had Patricia. The mood of the night had been set and Michael didn't ease up.

Emily offered drinks as they all sat uncomfortably in the sitting room. "Scotch on the rocks with a twist," ordered Michael fast and first.

"I'll help you with everyone's drinks," said Ashley.

"So, John," said Michael. "What is your line of work?" Michael began to interrogate John, which was apparent to the whole room. Occasionally, Martin answered on John's behalf, trying to show Michael that John was family and wouldn't be treated any differently.

"Michael, I've heard so much about your doctor skills. You're very good at the hospital," John said.

"Yes, I've a very good inspirational mentor," replied Michael smiling at Martin. The fake compliment disgusted everyone including Martin, but was lost on John. Michael had not interpreted John's presence as Emily's new boyfriend. He felt Ashley was second best and therefore his status had been lowered in this family. His mother treated him as second best as well. He blamed Ashley. Once again, noticing that John was seated next to Martin and Emily, Michael requested another drink.

"Are you having another alcoholic drink?" asked Ashley.

"I want to relax. Can't you drive us home tonight?" snarled Michael.

"I know you're not on call, so no worries," replied Ashley.

The Newells were growing wary of Michael. They knew he didn't usually drink, and he was getting almost aggressive in his behavior towards Ashley. Dinner was served earlier than planned.

Michael drank more than he ate. This wasn't the night he had planned! Michael had seduced Ashley to make Emily jealous. The whole underlying reason was access to Martin and the career progression it would bring. But nothing was working.

The table conversation flowed, with Michael only speaking if spoken to directly. Michael watched as Martin spoke fondly to John. *That should have been me,* he thought.

After dinner was eaten and the table cleared, Martin said that he was feeling unwell. Ashley said, in that case, they should leave. Michael wasn't happy to be leaving before John. He said goodbye to Martin and Patricia, but only nodded to Emily. He didn't acknowledge John at all.

As Ashley and Michael drove away, he yelled at her, unleashing his built-up fury.

"Michael! Don't speak to me like that! You made a complete fool of yourself tonight. I'll drive you home and then not contact you again. We are finished."

Michael was drunk yet felt stunned. Would "second best" Ashley really dump him? He lashed out and slapped Ashley across the face. Michael used the back of his hand and the hard blow caused Ashley to swerve the car. It was unexpected, shocking and completely unacceptable.

Ashley was clearly very shaken but she managed to continue driving the car. They drove home in stony silence.

Chapter Twenty-eight

It had been five months since Joseph had been shot. He still didn't know how it happened or how the bullets they'd removed from his body had come from his own gun. Previously, he'd been very fit and so he wasn't happy to still be using a walking cane. The bullets had been fired for maximum impact and he was grateful he could afford the best surgeons to repair his shattered bones. He was also grateful he wasn't in a wheelchair.

There had been numerous operations. He had resisted the urge to take some of his drugs for the pain. The fact that he could resist while in so much pain made him feel utter contempt for his clients. He knew of other drug dealers who had become drug addicts and their empires had fallen. Joseph was a very successful businessman and ran his business with protocols and balance sheets. He needed a clear head to lead and stay alive. He was tough enough to ride through the pain and so kept focused on the rewards.

As CEO of his legitimate business, he had called a board meeting to establish why the takings of one business were down. He had heard rumors, but he needed facts. As the owner of so many companies, Joseph was able to move money through the different companies until it became legal tender. His board members consisted of the type of professional people you would see on the board of any big corporation. Loyalty was key in this organization. The board members knew they would be sacked if theft or disloyalty were ever discovered. The stakes were high and the rewards even higher.

Once all the board members were seated, Joseph called the meeting to order. The first item on the agenda was the Foundation. He had crossed with them on many occasions and was getting over their involvement in his life. They were ruining his business.

"Slash, what have you found out?" asked Joseph.

"As you know, I found the man who you think shot you. You also know all attempts to get him, the girl, or that Lampoon guy have failed. That guy can identify me and, in return, everyone knows I work for you. He's still in prison but we can't get any more takers for the contract. The inmates say Lampoon is too street smart. There have been three deaths and no one wants money they'll never spend," reported Slash.

"We'll suspend the prison contract. Lampoon's court case is in the distance. Police have not come looking for you so we can address it later," said Joseph. "Next."

"Over the last month the takings are down to half. We're losing a lot of our drug-addicted clients. The Foundation has a successful detox program that is proving one hundred percent successful," said Slash. "The Foundation program has an entry exam of some sort. So far none of our dealers are passing the entry requirement. They are feeling the stress of losing clients they have taken a long time to groom. They don't want to be blamed for loss of profits."

"Good. Keep the pressure on the dealers. They'll have to source new clients. Have we warned the Foundation to cease the program?" asked Joseph.

"We have approached staff members and threatened them at night in their carpark. The staff members were very scared and said only the directors had the power to stop the program."

"No more warnings, I want the programmer gone. Will you take the contract?"

"No. I think the Foundation is jinxed. I'll contract an interstate recruit."

"Make it quick! The more successful the detox program, the more money I'm losing," replied Joseph.

* * *

Allan crouched in his hiding position, watching the lights in the Foundation building being turned off. His cell phone vibrated as he received a call. He knew the incoming number. "Yes, Slash?"

"You've had this contract for a week, what's the problem?"

"I know who the programmer is and I can see him lock up at night, but then he goes out a secret exit and I lose him. I can hit a director instead?" replied Allan.

"We want the programmer. Each day means more addicts cleaned and more money gone. You have one more day and then you've lost the contract."

"But, this is my reputation," said Allan.

"You have one more day to save face."

The following night Allan was back in the same location again and under pressure. This was his last night to succeed. This hit was proving to be challenging. From Allan's hidden position, he could watch the Foundation's carpark as staff left for the night. He noticed Patricia walking to her car and knew she was a director. Patricia didn't know that she had a red dot on her forehead.

Sorry lady, but you're the director paying my way, thought Allan as he prepared to squeeze the gun trigger. Just then, movement in the Foundation building caught his eye and he noticed Emily and John preparing to lock up.

Saved by the bell, thought Allan. He allowed Patricia to get into her car to drive away.

Allan had previously checked out all locations around the Foundation building, trying to locate a secret exit. Each night John had managed to disappear so it was now a process of elimination. There was only one more potential area and tonight Allan felt lucky. He picked up his items and moved to the area he was thinking of. He waited half an hour and then realized he had lost his opportunity, his contract and his reputation. Word would get out and this contract would double in price, but Allan's reputation would be worthless.

Allan walked to his car, opened the driver's door and sat in front of the steering wheel. Slash would be calling soon. He started the engine to drive to the pub. Rounding the corner near the hospital, a familiar face emerged and crossed the street. "You'll do," said Allan as he began to accelerate.

Chapter Twenty-nine

Patricia was woken up by the sound of the gate intercom. They were not expecting any visitors so she ran down to the monitor. She didn't recognize the car.

"This is the police. We're here to talk to Patricia Newell. Is she home?"

Patricia opened the gate and shouted through the house for Emily.

"What?" exclaimed Emily, shaken by her mother's panicked shout, made worse by her tiredness from minimal sleep.

"The police are here," replied Patricia as she ran to the front door.

"Hello Miss and Mrs Newell," Emily recognized the officers from her work at the Foundation. "We have met you before. I'm Sergeant Stewart and this is Constable Barndon. May we please come inside and sit down?"

Patricia began to shake. They were too formal to be here on business for the Foundation.

"We have very sad news for you. There is never an easy way to say it. There was an accident earlier tonight that involved Doctor Newell," said the detective, softly.

Patricia began to cry. "No, no! What happened?"

"Doctor Newell was hit by a car and couldn't to be revived."

Emily and Patricia exploded with grief, shouting and crying. They sat down, unable to move. The officers sat with the ladies offering them tissues and water.

"We are very sorry," said Sergeant Stewart.

"Doctor Newell was a very respected man so it's difficult news for us to deliver," said Constable Barndon.

After what felt like an eternity, Emily managed to refocus herself and hug Patricia, trying to absorb some of her pain. "What happened?" asked Emily.

"There was a hit and run about an hour ago. Doctor Newell was going to his work apartment and was crossing the road near the hospital. Medics ran out of the hospital and were quickly on location, but Doctor Newell was already deceased. The staff worked hard trying to save him. It was their admiration for your husband that kept them going, but they all knew it was too late."

The detectives didn't know any further details. There appeared to be no witnesses so it would be an investigative case.

* * *

John walked down the stairs after arriving via a portal upstairs. He had been in the city when he'd overheard the details. He knew Emily and Patricia would need his help. On seeing John, Patricia leaned forward and fainted before she could utter a single word. She missed hitting her head on any of the furniture and just slipped onto the floor. John lifted Patricia with ease, gently placing her back in her chair.

* * *

Emily now channeled her despair into attending to her mother and trying to understand how her wonderful father could be taken in such a senseless act. Emily lovingly patted Patricia's face and held some water to her lips to sip. Patricia looked at the police and let out a very long, painful scream. Her eyes were cascading tears and Emily noticed just how frail she looked.

Eventually the police left, assuming John was a relative or partner to Emily. Once the door was closed and they were left alone, they realized this was it – Martin was gone. Emily rang Ashley, but after trying to tell her the news, had to hand the phone to John. Ashley's screams could be heard very loudly.

"She's coming now," said John, handing Emily back her phone.

Emily shook her head and in a daze started to think about the great life times she'd shared with her dad. He'd always been there for her and when he had needed her most, she hadn't been there for him. She began to resent herself and then started to blame John. While John was protecting innocent people that night, her dad lay in the street dying. There were so many "what ifs," running through Emily's head. Emily helped Patricia to the bathroom and came back to wait with John. John remained calm throughout, not grieving at all. Emily grew angry. She did not want to spend centuries with a man with no heart.

"Just leave, John!" she said. "Don't come back. I don't want to be a part of your world anymore. You were in the city tonight so you had the chance to help my dad but you didn't." Emily's anger at the injustice and the devastating numbing loss was about to rip her heart in two. "You don't even care. Just leave!"

"Emily," said John, softly. "I'm sorry. Your father was very good to me; he's a very good person. I don't know how to show my sadness like you, but for the first time ever I feel a loss. I'm proud to say that your father was the best man I've ever met. I know I'll miss him." John walked away and disappeared through a portal.

Emily felt heavy in her heart. John had tried to express his feelings and his words were beautiful. Emily was caught between two worlds. She didn't want the life of a Purifier; she wanted her old life with her father.

"I heard your conversation with John," said Patricia. "I know you're upset Em, but don't forget your father in your grief. You father was very proud of you. He wouldn't be blaming you or John for what happened." Emily's sobs grew louder and Patricia comforted her. "Your dad saw your gift as a gift to society. He spent his life trying to help people, just as you can also do with your gift. He'll live on through you. You can continue the work he raised and prepared you for. He loved John and wanted John to be a part of his life as much as yours. This is going to be a long and very hard process. We have each other and we have Ashley. John may not be capable of showing his emotions just yet, but he's visibly very shocked. He could not identify it, but he loved your father, as much as your father loved him."

Emily stayed huddled in Patricia's arms. Ashley walked in and rushed over to Emily and Patricia and joined in the hug. The three women spent the very long night together, alternating between sobbing and sitting quietly remembering. Martin had been such an important part of their lives and was going to be terribly missed and long mourned.

"Martin was proud of both of you; he was proud of us," said Pat during one of their silent intervals. A death is a terrible loss to anyone but, for these three ladies, Martin was a particularly special person. The impact to his family, friends, work and society was going to be huge.

* * *

Even though Emily had tried to banish John, he hadn't quite left. He was inside a portal and had stayed hidden but present with the ladies all night. He was learning about his emotions through Emily and he felt that he needed to be with his family tonight. John felt such an emptiness through the sorrow, devastation and physical loss of Martin and knew he would genuinely miss him.

Chapter Thirty

Emily had spent two nights and one whole day cocooned in the house with Ashley and Patricia. They talked constantly about Martin, then they spoke about funeral arrangements. Patricia would occasionally mention that she missed seeing John around the house. Ashley now understood just how close John had become to the family.

Emily was still trying to make sense of and rationalize her hurt, anger, life purpose and her connection with John. So this morning, leaving Ashley and Patricia still asleep in their beds, she had jumped out of bed very early, ate a quick breakfast and then gone for a morning run. Her mind was distracted by the music blaring through her headphones and the burn of her muscles. She had spent the whole night thinking of John and her dad. She admired how her dad had embraced John in order to secure a future for Emily and how in her hurt, she blamed John and had dismissed him. It occurred to her she was trying to teach John about emotions and hadn't really given him a chance.

As she circled back towards the house, she pulled out her phone. "Hi John," she said, unsure of his reaction.

"Hi Emily," replied John.

With his unlearnt skill of expressing emotion, Emily was unable to determine if John was happy or disappointed to hear from her. "Can we talk?" she asked.

"Over the phone or in person?"

"Whatever suits you," replied Emily as John tapped her on her shoulder. Emily smiled and hugged John. He awkwardly hugged back, not realizing that Emily was happy to see him. "I'm so sorry John," she said as she pulled away.

"It's OK. I think I know why you don't want to be a Purifier anymore. And I'm sorry I was unable to help Martin. I've thought about him a lot since the accident."

"It wasn't your fault. I was wrong to blame you. You did help my dad to understand and accept my history. He accepted you into our family and so do I. I should never have told you to leave that night. Were you alright?" she said.

John half smiled. "I was with you, Ashley and Patricia. I stayed in my portal, out of sight. When I could, I would emerge to speak with Patricia and she explained a lot to me. She said you would want to see me again and I just had to wait until you were ready. You are really close to Patricia and Ashley and I'll learn my lessons to help you in the future."

"Yes John. That was part of the hurt I was feeling; the reality that I'll outlive everyone who I love and, obviously, the deep pain of losing my wonderful father."

"I was thinking about the lessons you have been helping me with. Maybe I can show you something that I discussed with Martin," said John.

"OK. Will we be walking the streets again?" she asked.

"No, not this time. Martin and I were talking about your world. My mission is to locate evil but never change the course of history. Martin came up with many ideas to expand on your life path and use your skills for a greater purpose. I would like to show you some of the benefits to our skills – how and who we help."

"Martin said I should first start by taking you to Africa. The hospital has a mission there and you know Ryan is already there. If we leave now, I promise to have you back by lunchtime."

Emily tried to laugh, but with so many stories about Martin, her heart was still too heavy, so she settled for a smile. "Arh, the portal. Now that is something I definitely don't want to lose. Let me go tell Mom. Since the accident she likes to know where we all are."

They had reached the house, so Emily ran up to Patricia's room and told her she was going to Africa and returning by lunch today. It certainly lightened the mood.

"I see you and John are friends again," she said. "He was looking after us the whole time. He didn't abandon us. He didn't know why Martin had died."

"Thank you, Mom. I thought about what you said, and you were right. Dad prepared me and in honor of him, I must continue." Emily kissed Patricia on her forehead and ran back to John.

Emily was beginning to feel she shared the same friendship with John as she did Ashley. His social awkwardness was endearing; he was funny and he was trying to embrace his emotions.

* * *

The portal took longer this time with the wind speedily brushing their faces. Emily departed the portal with her hair looking like it had been in a wind tunnel.

"Do you have a mirror?" asked John, laughing.

"No, why?"

John shrugged his shoulders and led Emily to an entrance. As they walked through the doors of the orphanage, they passed several people who appeared to look especially at Emily with surprised faces. John finally told Emily that the portal had made her hair stand up very high and was all over the place. They both laughed and Emily was impressed with John's growing sense of humor. Emily patted her hair down into some semblance of order and asked John why they were at an orphanage.

"Emily, inside there are hundreds of children who were abandoned by their parents, for many different reasons. These children are blank slates. A child doesn't have an outline until they reach maturity. These children are disheartened. They love when volunteers visit, but a visit doesn't bring hope. Our skills can bring them the hope and love that usually only a loving parent can provide. You have learnt the value of your hands and their touch. You have allowed some people to reassess their life. You provided what they needed, which in those instances was clarity and purpose. I encourage you to interact with these children and embrace them. Watch and learn what you can achieve."

They entered the orphanage rooms and Emily noticed they were not large. The furniture was sparse and there were minimal toys, not even enough for one toy per child. Most of the children were kicking a ball around outside in a dirty yard. Emily immediately felt the loneliness and despair. As the children noticed the visitors, they smiled and quickly came over to meet them.

Emily did as John instructed and cuddled the children, one by one. She focused on her touch providing a feeling happiness that morphed into security and love. The children received hope and a chance to embrace life. The room no longer felt lonely as the children played joyfully.

John called Emily outside, and within minutes, they walked back inside carrying a crate full of toys, and other crates full of clothing, fruit and bedding.

Emily felt bewildered and looked at John.

"Yes, Emily, we can do this. We can help people, by not just stopping evil. Unfortunately, we cannot change the course of history and can only help on a small needs basis. There is only ever one of us here, and our missions are based on saving the good people from the evil."

The children each selected a toy of their own. There were smiles and laughter, as the children played with a new sense of hope, possible dreams and now a new belonging. Emily and John waved their goodbyes, left the orphanage and took a small portal to visit Ryan. They didn't leave the portal, so they weren't visible. Emily felt such pride watching Ryan be the great doctor he always wanted to be. Emily knew she would revisit again soon.

She whispered to John and the portal moved to the medical supply room. As expected the medical supplies were nearly gone, so John created at least twenty items of each necessity. The hospital would have to monitor the resources, so an oversupply could encourage a black market.

The portal took John and Emily outside. "Ready to return home now, Emily? Can you see there are so many good things you can do? It's all about balance. You may be here for four hundred years, but imagine how many children you can give hope to. You're already working with the Foundation clients to try and help them before they end up at the hospital where your father worked endlessly to save them. Now in a different way, you can help more people. This is what your father and I spoke of. He told me he always knew you would make a difference in the world. He wanted this for you. But, it's for you to embrace if you want it in your life."

Emily cried; it was soothing for her to learn of the conversations Martin had with John about her. "John, I want to continue my training and not only because of my father. I want to continue it for me. This is what I want to do. I got so much value out of today."

They walked around the corner and immediately disappeared from Africa. They walked out of the portal and were on a beach in the Bahamas.

"John, what are we doing here!" exclaimed Emily, looking around with delight.

"I just wanted to show you a beautiful part of your world and how important you are to make sure it stays that way," said John, sincerely.

Emily laughed, as she took of her shoes and walked into the water. They walked and talked, just as before, reigniting their common goal. Emily took a moment to follow up on John's training. She wanted to find out what John had learnt from the last few days.

"Well, after watching you, Patricia and Ashley, I can now say that crying women make me feel uncomfortable and really lost," said John, too bluntly but with honesty.

Emily burst into laughter. "Oh John! Your innocence is so delightful. Sometimes I hesitate to change you." She paused. "John, trust me, that is something you don't tell a grieving woman."

Emily and John then walked back through the portal and into the Newell estate.

"Thank you, John," said Emily. She suddenly felt a lot better.

Chapter Thirty-one

The funeral arrangements for Martin had been made with a lot of love and care. Hundreds of mourners were expected to attend and pay their respects. In lieu of flowers, the Newell's had requested that the money to be donated to a charity. The funeral would be a tribute to a great man. The hospital had insisted on paying. Patricia accepted the funeral costs as a gift and knew she would donate to the hospital in the future.

Alexis had rung last night to offer her condolences to her friends, Ashley and Emily. She apologized saying she was on location and wouldn't be able to attend Martin's funeral, but that she would be thinking about them tomorrow. Both girls agreed the friendship with Alexis had been the best gift from Michael.

The funeral cars were due to arrive at ten o'clock. Emily, Patricia and Ashley would travel in one car and Chadi and John in a second car. Chadi could easily have travelled in the first car, but there needed to be transport available to explain John's mode of transport from the church to the wake. Chadi was invited to be a part of Martin's farewell. He was also invited to sit in the front pew with the family. Patricia had asked Chadi to leave the hospital CEO driver position so he could remain on as their driver at the Foundation. Martin wouldn't have wanted Chadi to lose his job.

The funeral cars arrived on time and the drive was very somber. Each person was deep in their own thoughts about Martin. The sun shone brightly as Emily looked out the car window.

"Doesn't the weather know this should be a gloomy day?" said Emily, reaching for her sunglasses.

"I just want to get through today and get on with our lives," said Patricia. None of them were looking forward to this last goodbye to Martin.

As they arrived at the church, in the car procession behind the hearse, the large crowd of people parted leaving room for the family to enter together. The mourners looked on in support, their loss evident on their faces. It soon became obvious that everyone from the huge crowd wouldn't be able to fit into the church, so the PA system was switched on so the outside speakers could broadcast the ceremony.

* * *

Michael had arrived early with Oliver and had found a seat inside the church. Oliver wanted to pay his respects to Emily and to Martin who he had heard so many remarkable things about in the finance world. Michael watched the family enter the church and walk to the front pew. He saw Chadi and John sit with the family and was furious that his rightful seat was given to someone else. He was obsessed with mourning the loss of his career prospects, rather than Martin the doctor. Michael had genuinely liked Martin and always admired him, but sitting behind the family and watching John, he felt betrayed.

* * *

As the ceremony progressed and with so many people wanting to say a few words about what a great man Martin had been,

Ashley and Emily were busy supporting Patricia as well as themselves. John was sitting next to Ashley and although Ashley was glad she knew him well from the Foundation project, she did wonder how John had built such a strong relationship with the family in such a brief period of time. *Seriously, who is this man?* thought Ashley.

Emily delivered a powerful eulogy. Her words were emotional, full of love and moved everyone to tears. Patricia sobbed uncontrollably and Ashley inconsolable. Ashley was unable to watch Emily through her tears and unconsciously grabbed John's leg, seeking the emotional strength she needed to support herself and Patricia.

* * *

John noticed Ashley's hand on his leg and knew she needed strength. Watching Ashley's pain and hearing Emily's words, began to have an effect on John's emotions. He could feel the pain through Ashley and warm tears began to run down his cheeks. He held Ashley's hand on his leg and tried to support her. He found he now needed support as much as she did. John was surprised by the emotional pain he felt. He had never been more aware of himself and in tune with his body.

He placed his arm around Ashley's shoulder in a comforting gesture and whispered into Ashley's ear, "He was such a good man. He'll be missed." Ashley's tears eased and her sobs subsided as she felt comforted by John. John was again surprised he felt the same emotion. *Why am I feeling everything she's feeling?* thought John as he let go of all contact with Ashley and continued to wipe away his own tears.

* * *

Emily finished her eulogy and walked back to her mother. She looked at John as he was wiping away a tear and a flood of emotion overcame her. Emily realized the power of Martin's loss.

The funeral ceremony ended and the family members moved outside to be available to the mourners as they left the church.

* * *

When Michael approached the family, it was obvious he was hurting but was struggling with his thoughts. "Sorry for your loss, Patricia," he said with tears welling up again. "Dr Newell was an inspiration and I'll truly miss him.

"Thank you, Michael," Patricia replied. "Martin had high hopes for you. He would love to see you fulfil your potential."

Michael began to shed tears again, just thinking that Dr Newell had recognized his potential and spoke positively about him. "Thank you, Patricia," Michael managed to reply. He next moved along the line to Ashley.

"Sorry to hear of Martin's loss. I hope you're OK," he said with minimal sympathy. He had seen Ashley with John and could not move past his inner struggle of feeling he was being replaced. He was here to say goodbye to Martin his mentor, and to his chance of furthering his career.

Michael avoided John and moved reluctantly on to talk to Emily. Emily would know about his breakup with Ashley and he wasn't sure of his welcome.

"Hi Emily, I'm sorry to hear of your loss. It's a great loss to everyone."

"Thank you. How are you?" asked Emily, surprising Michael.

"It's difficult, I'll miss him greatly," said Michael. Starting to feel the truth of his statement, he began to cry. "Your father was one of the few people who believed in me."

Emily reached out her hands to embrace him. Michael looked up at Emily, overcome by grief. "I let him down. I'm sorry Emily for everything. I have to leave." He was inconsolable. This was the first time he actually thought of Martin as an actual person and not for himself. He now realized his career was nothing. He had truly lost a wonderful man who he'd admired.

* * *

Emily lent in and whispered into Michael's ear. "Michael, you have a chance now to be the man and the doctor my father always saw in you." She kissed him on the cheek and he walked away.

John made his way over to Emily. "Michael is flashing yellow. That was very nice of you," he said.

"My father always believed in him and now I do too," replied Emily. She hugged John and John returned the embrace. Funerals always evoke a lot of emotion. "John, you're my dearest friend, will be my longest friend and I love you for that."

"You're an excellent teacher and I too love you," replied John with feeling and not just words. "But I don't think I like the crying. For the first time, I feel emotionally drained."

Patricia, Ashley and Emily re-invited everyone back to the wake at the Newell estate.

"It was a beautiful ceremony," said Chadi, wiping tears from his eyes.

"Yes, Chadi. A beautiful celebration for a beautiful life," said Patricia.

Nearly seven hundred people attended the wake. The food and drink flowed and everyone commented that Dr Newell always threw a great party. Emily and Ashley didn't leave Patricia's side. They were able to watch the greatest party unfold, without the greatest host present.

"Dad would be so proud," said Emily.

"Yes. He loved a party and he would be so proud of us and especially you and Ashley. I love you both so much, I could not have got through this without you." Patricia cried with tears of sadness, joy and pride.

"We love you so much Mom and we could not have got through this without you," said Emily, throwing her arms around Patricia, with Ashley joining in with the embrace.

Chapter Thirty-two

Martin's death had an impact on so many people. Michael was surprised at the profound effect it was having on him. Since the funeral, Michael had reassessed the choices he had made in his life and had asked himself, like the great Dr Martin Newell, how he wanted to be remembered. Michael realized that he needed to right his wrongs and make better life choices. He had originally wanted to be a great surgeon and due to some negative outside influences had lost his way.

Fortunatley, he was still young and so, now at the crossroads of his life, it was time to redefine his life purpose and put a positive plan into action. Michael contacted Ryan in Africa and found that Ryan had no hard feelings towards him or Ashley as he was so engrossed in a higher mission. He said while his life was hard, it was very rewarding. He told Michael there was always work available for him and if he did decide to come to Africa to bring plenty of medical supplies.

Michael now felt grateful he'd been overlooked for Dr Newell's position. It wasn't his passion after all. Perhaps it had been his mother's, but not his. It was time to reclaim his life and shake off the influences that were holding him back. Michael contacted Ryan again and said he would come and to let him know the exact supplies he needed sent over.

That night Michael met his father at the Country Club to discuss his new life mission. He respected his father and would deeply miss him. Michael felt that Oliver was the only person who genuinely loved Michael for himself. He had never minded about his career choice, income or social standing.

"Hi Michael," said Oliver greeting him warmly.

"Thanks for meeting me, Dad." They sat down together. Michael ordered a drink. It would be the first and last time Michael drank at the club. "I'm leaving for Africa. I want to begin afresh. I'm not happy with my life. I would be more fulfilled working as a doctor in Africa."

"I'm proud of you," replied Oliver, standing up to hug his son.

They discussed that Oliver would still be responsible for Michael's investment wealth and future finances. By the end of their meeting, it was also decided Michael would sell his car and furnishings to buy the medical supplies. His investment portfolio would fund his time in Africa or depending on the future, to make a new start in life. Michael knew his parents didn't talk, so he didn't bother to mention he wanted to tell Susan personally.

With his finances sorted out and having established a great relationship with his dad, Michael gave his notice at work and insisted on confidentiality. He would advise Ashley himself when the time was right. Michael contacted his brother Samuel to meet him for lunch. Samuel wasn't available to meet Michael for a week, but was happy to see him. Michael told Samuel that he was a great brother and it was time to say goodbye. Samuel was shocked that Michael would forgo his prestige and fortune and go and work in Africa.

The brothers discussed this during their conversation and, while Samuel just could not fathom or understand it, Michael realized the influence his mother had over all of their lives. He asked Samuel not to tell Susan as he wanted to tell her personally and it would probably be just before he flew out. Samuel promised and the brothers said their goodbyes. Samuels' final words to Michael were not to wish him success or congratulate him on his choice but, rather, to say, "I hope you can still see all the movies Alexis will star in."

* * *

It was now three weeks since Martin's funeral and Michael had completed his work notice, sold his car and furnishing, sent the medical supplies to Ryan and put his apartment onto the rental market. Michael felt he was moving to Africa for good, but just needed the safety net of his apartment rented rather than sold. He could always sell it later. He was due to fly out tomorrow so he'd had arranged to meet Susan today.

Michael drove the rental car to Susan's home. As he knocked on the door – probably for the last time – he tried to analyze his thoughts and feelings at not seeing his mother again. There was absolutely nothing. She was so shallow and he really would not miss her. He was ushered in and went over to kiss her hello.

"Hi Michael, what was so important I had to miss my meeting today? Why do you have your doctor's bag?" asked Susan.

"Hi Mom. Thank you for meeting me. I have big news and I could not leave the bag in the car."

"Did you get the CEO position?" asked Susan, excitedly.

"No Mom. My big news is that I'm going to be the doctor I always wanted to be and have thrown in all the trappings of this life to go to work in Africa. While I know you're disappointed by this, I'll also wanted tell you I'm taking the love of my life who has always supported my decision and given me unconditional love."

"Your brother was always so successful. It's extremely disappointing. I'd hoped you would be a famous plastic surgeon or, at least, the hospital CEO. You seemed changed over the past few months so I began to think you had the same passion as your brother. But clearly I was mistaken. Who is the love of your life?" asked Susan, with little care.

"You'll remember our old neighbors Jake and Lauren. Well, I have always loved Lauren and now she's now divorced from Jake, it's time it was the two of us," replied Michael proudly.

"She'll suit you. Two losers. I never liked her and now I know why," snarled Susan.

"Anyway Mom, thank you for your understanding, I fly out tomorrow and this is our final goodbye."

"You were always a disappointment. You'll fail in Africa and fail with Lauren … just like everything else." She drove her disgust into Michael's breaking heart. Susan turned to walk to her bedroom. Michael followed; he didn't want those final words to be the last ones he ever spoke to his mother. He wanted a positive start to his new life. Once again, Susna was trying to strip that away. He hugged her and whispered, "Goodbye, Mom."

As Michael turned and walked away, a weight lifted off his shoulders. Michael was free of Susan. He couldn't see it, but Michael suspected Susan might be having a few heart problems just about now. He patted his doctors bag. Michael smiled as he drove back to spend his last night in New York with Lauren. There were two more endings that still needed to be played out. He picked up his phone.

"Hi Ashley, I've rung to say goodbye. I want to apologize for the way our relationship started and ended."

"Michael, what do you mean goodbye?" asked Ashley.

Michael explained to Ashley how professionally he had lost his way. He became obsessed with chasing the corporate career and he was going to follow Ryan to Africa to practice medicine to help people and live in his passion. Dr Newell's death had given him the wakeup call that he needed. Dr Newell was his mentor and the greatest humanitarian he ever knew. He also wanted to leave a legacy he could be proud of.

"Actually, there's one more thing I want to tell you. I'm going to Africa with the love of my life. Her name is Lauren and she has been in my life for ten years. She was never good enough for my mother so I had to have a second life with her and she has loved me unconditionally."

"I thought Lauren was in the hall far too many times when I came to your place, but thank you Michael for your honesty. You're happy and Ryan is happy so it's all worked out in the end. I sincerely wish you a great life with Lauren by your side. If I can ever help, you know how to contact me."

"Thank you. You're also a great person and a great doctor so I also wish you a great life. Goodbye."

Michael then rang Emily who was his final goodbye. Michael explained his new life path and wanted to let Emily know that his decision was a tribute to Dr Newell. The funeral was what had made Michael question his legacy. Emily congratulated Michael and wished him enormous success.

Chapter Thirty-three

Life without Martin was still raw; it would take some time for everyone to adapt to not having him around. The Foundation become the central location for Patricia, Emily, Ashley and John. They all worked there daily in different capacities, with Ashley continuing to work at the hospital as well.

Patricia buried herself in her work to avoid her grief. Emily kept the Foundation work to a minimum as she was still completing her residency, learning her skills, training John and being a friend to Ashley. They all supported each other, with Patricia as the central focus. John was still emotionally naïve. He had made considerable progress but he needed to learn some tact. His answers took people by surprise on many occasions. Ashley was now socializing with Emily and John, so his training was now in real time, with limited assistance from Emily.

The unsolved case of Martin's death and the details of Rogers case had caused concern. John had placed a protection over Patricia, the Foundation and the Newell house. Ashley was unaware and would remain so, until John advised otherwise. Emily encouraged Ashley to stay at the house, but Ashley preferred to stay in the city when working night shift, so Emily would stay with her. Everyone was worried that Ashley was now in danger by association.

The Foundation had managed to successfully implement its drug rehab program. Entry into the life-skill courses was increasingly in demand and the clients were preparing for a good future filled with possibilities. Emily's increase in street walking had given people a chance to change their lives. Many people wanted to embrace the offer, so the Foundation opened a department in memory of Martin. Social workers were employed to support people seeking help to improve themselves. The success rate demonstrated how wonderful Emily's skills were.

John would still walk the streets and worked with Roger, visiting him as much as possible. Roger had been in jail for two months. After the initial attacks, he was totally ignored and left alone by his fellow inmates. No matter what the inmates had promised him, Roger knew life outside of jail was where his future would improve.

John wanted Roger to know he was never alone or forgotten and to ensure Roger didn't change his outline. It was a case of so far, so good. Roger was very keen for a normal life with a job, a home and the possibility of a family. Life in jail was tolerable. He had shelter, warmth, food and a bathroom available whenever he needed it. When you have been homeless, you can be very flexible and always grateful for these comforts.

Roger's case was due to be allocated a trial date. Even though most people knew Roger was innocent, there was still the task of accumulating evidence and finding the guilty party. A man had been killed and even though he was a homeless man, his life was still valuable and someone had to be accountable.

Slash and Joseph were monitoring the situation and their informants had advised there were no evidence and nothing to worry about. Martin's death was still being investigated to establish if it had been an accident or a deliberate act. If murder was established, it wouldn't be so easily dismissed and Slash and Joseph could only hope the professional contract was never linked back to them.

Roger didn't need to attend court personally for his trial date as the state was reducing all unnecessary costs. John attended court where the judge set a trial date to start in three months' time and with the usual delays, it meant five months as a minimum. John didn't apply for bail as Roger didn't have a fixed address. Roger was formally denied bail and ordered to remain in jail.

Life had improved with John in his life and Roger felt confident that he could expect more good luck. He know that John, Emily and the Foundation could be trusted. John was still in contact with the other Johns and was relaying messages through them to his home contacts, trying to get the information vital to Emily surviving a transit through the main portal and a visit to his world.

From the information he'd received and the data he'd processed, it did seem as though Emily had enough of her birth father's genetics to survive a visit to his world. He was also told the King had identified Emily's birth father and would be able to introduce her to him.

Emily was asking more and more detailed questions about his world and John knew she was looking for something to fill the hole in her life. Martin's death had made Emily more aware that she would outlive all her friends and family. So she was keen to know she had somewhere to go when she could no longer live on Earth.

John and Emily still enjoyed their time together. He was the only person Emily could expose her true self too. They shared stories with each other, and Emily wanted to know more about John's world. She struggled to disconnect the human life to the Purifier life. In John's world, the "entities" were star twinkles; they were able to identify each other without a human body. However, Emily could not envision this concept.

"John," said Emily. "Would I be able to identify you in your world?"

"I'm not sure as this is so new to me. I feel that you would still see my human form, but I don't know if you would see anyone else in a body."

Emily had not asked much about his world until now. "Do you have partners and families?"

"Some do. When people are ready for a family, you go to something like a shop. There are three sections. One section is for the scenario where a female wants to raise a child alone and is looking for an anonymous male activation; second section is for a partner to raise a family together and the third section is where the female leaves a gift for a sole father. My father wanted me so he went to the third section, identified with the female half, activated my male half and then he raised me on his own."

"So, you don't have a mother?" asked Emily.

"No. I was a gift to my father, left to him by a female twinkle," he said. "Our living quarters are like the homes you're familiar with here. We see them differently to you. When we return from an Earth visit, we see how beautiful our world is and appreciate the beauty we call home."

"John, I want to go there, I have an urge to see where I am from. I want to know how my biological dad could father me. Do you know if I can breathe and have normal body functions?" asked Emily.

"Your blood has oxygen so breathing will be OK. I think your body would adapt as you're only going to be away for two weeks, maybe three," answered John, still very unclear on how it would work. "You'll feel like it's only two days, but according to the Earth rotation it will be two weeks. We also have beautiful clear water and we could create any food you want, whenever you are hungry."

Emily wondered if John's world would accept her, considering that they hated earthly missions, thinking humans were all evil. She also desperately wanted to know why her father left and why he never came back. She was grateful for her parents; she just wanted to be able to understand his thought processes and if he'd loved her mother.

"Is my father still alive?" asked Emily.

"Based on our longevity and your age, I feel confident in saying yes. My world wants to understand how he was able to create you," said John. "We understand how humans are made, but we don't understand how your bodies work."

"Can I stay longer than two weeks?" asked Emily.

"Once we do the first trip, I hope you'll feel very comfortable and will be able to stay for longer periods."

"How is the home portal different to the other ones we use?" asked Emily.

"The home portal is in a city laneway. We must go to it. Cars can drive along the laneway and not interfere with the portal. It's only tangible when one of us needs to use it. When we enter the portal, it's still very quick and timeless when inside. When we get home, it's like your bus station. You'll come through a destination exit and when coming back here, you'll enter through the correct entrance. We go to many various locations and must enter the correct portal."

"John, I want go. I need to go away and find myself. Can we go soon?" asked Emily.

"We have completed the data; they are ready for you whenever you feel ready to go," replied John.

Emily and John decided it was time for her to go and visit John's home. He would be excited to show her around as she had done for him. In his mind, he had already planned the places he wanted to show her.

* * *

Before leaving, Emily had to make sure Patricia and Ashley would be safe. Protections were already in place, but because Emily could not stay in the apartment with Ashley or be with her at all, she asked Ashley to take time off work to care for Patricia.

"Ashley, please just stay with Mom and work with her at the Foundation. She cannot be alone. She'll need you," asked Emily.

"Em, you and your family were there for me when I needed you. Patricia is like my mother so of course I'll take time off to be with her," replied Ashley.

"I love you Ash," said Emily, hugging Ashley. "I'll see you in two to three weeks' time. Thank you for understanding."

Without any hesitation, Patricia agreed that Emily should visit John's world and Ashley would stay with her. Since Martin's sudden death, Patricia was obsessive about protecting the girls. Emily wouldn't have left Patricia if Ashley wasn't with her.

The arrangements were now in place. Patricia had Ashley and Ashley had Patricia. The day arrived and to continue with the façade, Emily explained to Ashley that she had arranged a bag transfer previously.

Goodbyes were said all round, as John and Emily got into Chadi's car and waved farwell. They then made their way down the drive and towards the portal.

"Emily, there is so much ahead of us. So many new skills and travels."